So many times
James had thought of her.

He had set out more than once to find Kelly, but each time had come back empty-handed. Now it was as if she'd never left. As if everything was the same.

Except for the child...

"Belinda Barnes delivers everything you want in a romance—a heart-tugging story filled with warm, wonderful characters."
                                         —Martha Shields, award-winning author

Dear Reader,

This June—traditionally the month of brides, weddings and the promise of love everlasting—Silhouette Romance also brings you the possibility of being a star! Check out the details of this special promotion in each of the six happily-ever-afters we have for you.

In *An Officer and a Princess*, Carla Cassidy's suspenseful conclusion to the bestselling series ROYALLY WED: THE STANBURYS, Princess Isabel calls on her former commanding officer to help rescue her missing father. Karen Rose Smith delights us with a struggling mom who refuses to fall for *Her Tycoon Boss* until the dynamic millionaire turns up the heat! In *A Child for Cade* by reader favorite Patricia Thayer, Cade Randall finds that his first love has kept a precious secret from him....

Talented author Alice Sharpe's latest offering, *The Baby Season*, tells of a dedicated career woman tempted by marriage and motherhood with a rugged rancher and his daughter. In *Blind-Date Bride*, the second book of Myrna Mackenzie's charming twin duo, the heroine asks a playboy billionaire to ward off the men sent by her matchmaking brothers. And a single mom decides to tell the man she has always loved that he has a son in Belinda Barnes's heartwarming tale, *The Littlest Wrangler*.

Next month be sure to return for two brand-new series— the exciting DESTINY, TEXAS by Teresa Southwick and the charming THE WEDDING LEGACY by Cara Colter. And don't forget the triumphant conclusion to Patricia Thayer's THE TEXAS BROTHERHOOD, along with three more wonderful stories!

Happy Reading!

Mary-Theresa Hussey

Mary-Theresa Hussey
Senior Editor

Please address questions and book requests to:
Silhouette Reader Service
U.S.: 3010 Walden Ave., P.O. Box 1325, Buffalo, NY 14269
Canadian: P.O. Box 609, Fort Erie, Ont. L2A 5X3

The Littlest Wrangler

Belinda Barnes

SILHOUETTE *Romance*®

Published by Silhouette Books

America's Publisher of Contemporary Romance

To my editor, Tina Colombo, with heartfelt thanks
and appreciation for your insight and gentle guidance

To Rox, Kathie and Janet for your unwavering support

To Kristi, Sandy, Terri and Virginia
for your endless patience and creative perception

 SILHOUETTE BOOKS

ISBN 0-373-19527-3

THE LITTLEST WRANGLER

Visit Silhouette at www.eHarlequin.com

Printed in U.S.A.

Books by Belinda Barnes

Silhouette Romance

His Special Delivery #1491
The Littlest Wrangler #1527

BELINDA BARNES

A romantic at heart, Romance Writers of America's 1999 Golden Heart winner Belinda Barnes grew up in Sand Springs, Oklahoma, on the banks of the Arkansas River, where she dreamed of faraway lands, castles and princes. Though Texas is not all that far away, it is there Belinda found her prince.Together in their two-story castle they have raised two sons, a daughter and a menagerie of pets, including dogs, cats, tropical fish, turtles, hamsters, ferrets.With sons whose interests run the gamut from bull riding to racing cars and motorcycles, Belinda is more than ready for her daughter's more sedate passions of dancing, singing and acting.

Belinda lives in Elm Mott, Texas, with her husband, her daughter and spoiled cat, Precious. In addition to fiction, she is published in magazine and book-length nonfiction. In her spare time she enjoys clogging, painting, reading, country-and-western music, dancing, fishing, scuba diving, camping and getting together with other writers.

Belinda loves to hear from readers. Write to her at P.O. Box 1165, Elm Mott, Texas 76640.

SILHOUETTE MAKES YOU A STAR!
Feel like a star with Silhouette.
Look for the exciting details of our new contest inside all of these fabulous Silhouette novels:

Chapter One

She'd grown up in hand-me-downs, had a baby alone and left the only man she had ever loved, but *this* was the hardest thing Kelly Mathews had ever done.

"James, this is Will. Your son."

No, that wasn't right, either.

She pulled her hand away from the doorknob to James Scott's equine veterinary clinic and marched back to her truck, her baby braced on her hip. She couldn't face the father of her child until she had it right. But what could she possibly say to make him understand why she hadn't told him he had a child?

She wouldn't lie. A lie is what had gotten her into this whole mess. Well, not exactly a lie so much as withholding the truth. Not telling James about Will before now had been a doozy of a mistake. It certainly wasn't the first one she'd ever made, but most definitely the biggest, second only to falling in love with Dr. James Scott. Her best friend.

Kelly's head pounded as Will wriggled, wanting

down. A wave of dizziness washed over her, forcing her to lean against the dented front fender of her truck. She tightened her hold on her child and tried to rein in her escalating fear that something was terribly wrong with her. Something that might take her from her son.

She pushed off from the faded-blue pickup and crossed the thick carpet of grass, lush and green from Texas's spring rains. If she didn't keep moving, she'd fall asleep on her feet. And she had to talk to James before that happened.

It was now or never.

Kelly sucked in a deep breath and squared her shoulders. As she pushed open the office door, she vowed her sweet baby's future would include his father.

As she took one step inside the veterinary clinic, her gaze settled on James standing across the room, head down, making an entry in a file. Memories of their one night together rushed at her, followed by the pain of all the lonely nights that had come after. Tears of what might have been stung her eyes, but she blinked them away, determined to see this through for her baby's sake.

James wore faded jeans, scarred boots and spurs, an indication he was probably on his way to the rodeo. The trophy buckle he'd won three years ago glistened against the denim shirt that covered his washboard abdomen, a sure sign he intended to do a little honky-tonking after his ride.

Even after all this time she still hated that buckle. It served as a neon light, flaunting his need to compete, his need to take foolish risks and avoid commitment. It also served as a reminder of why she'd had to leave, when in his arms was the only place she'd ever wanted to be.

She tried not to stare at James, but found herself looking at where his jeans met his boots. Then her gaze traveled up the muscled length of his long legs. Everything about the man—his confident stance and his angular jaw—screamed Bad Boy.

He hadn't changed.

And neither had the way he set her heart to pounding.

Kelly met his dark gaze. His face mirrored his surprise. For a long moment he said nothing but watched her with eyes the color of warm whiskey kissed by the Texas sun, eyes that touched her as thoroughly as his hands once had. He appraised her in a leisurely manner, eliciting unguarded feelings she'd given in to once, feelings she knew she shouldn't acknowledge. But it had been so long since she'd last seen him, and she had missed him so.

What a fool she'd been to think she could waltz in here and see James again and be okay. Well, she wasn't okay. And she didn't know if she ever would be.

"Well, I'll be damned." He dropped the folder and pen on a nearby desk and sauntered toward her, his lips turning up in a devilishly sexy smile, the same smile that had captured her heart. "It's about time you showed up again."

She wondered if James would still be smiling once he learned why she'd returned and if he would give her a chance to explain.

As though reading her mind, he bent to glance at Will. "Hey, buddy. How are you doing?"

Their son hunched one shoulder and buried his face in the curve of Kelly's neck.

She gave Will a reassuring squeeze. "He's a little shy."

James straightened and sent her a questioning look. "Who's this little fella?"

The sound of the air conditioner, the faint country music, served as a backdrop to his sudden silence while he stood waiting, watching, thinking only God knew what. She struggled to contain her anxiety.

"Kelly?" He tilted her chin with his forefinger and looked into her eyes.

She didn't want to tell him, didn't want to see the anger on his face. But most of all, she couldn't bear the thought of hurting him any more than she already had.

Reminding herself why she'd returned, she forced back her apprehension. "This is Will, someone I want you to know. H-he's my son."

Something like disappointment clouded James's eyes. "So you're married?"

"No. Will's two years old. He was born the fifth of May, two years ago."

She watched him digest that, could see the wheels turning in his head as he mentally did the math. And she waited.

Fear made her tremble. Fear of what he would say, of the effect on her son. Had she made a wrong decision over two years ago? No, not about leaving. She'd had no choice. But she should have told James about Will a long time ago. He'd had a right to know.

Kelly locked her knees against the weariness that threatened to buckle her legs. She prayed James wouldn't blame their child for what she had done. She prayed that he would grow to love Will. And she prayed he never discovered that, even after everything that had happened between them, after what she'd done, her feelings for him had never changed.

James's smile faded. His eyes narrowed in question, shifting from her to Will, then back. "Are you telling me—"

"Will is your child."

His child.

James Scott stood frozen. He had to remind himself to breathe. His head buzzed as if he'd taken a hard fall off the back of a bronc. The country music playing on the radio behind him faded into the background as her words hung in the air between them.

If he'd seen even a hint of a smile, he would suspect this to be one of the pranks they'd always played on each other, but the fear and exhaustion in Kelly's eyes told him otherwise.

Her betrayal twisted his gut into a tight knot. "Why, Kelly? What made you think you had the right to keep this from me?"

She flinched. "I didn't think—"

"You've got *that* right. You *didn't think* or you would have known how I'd feel, what I'd say."

"If you'll just give me a chance to explain—"

"Why should I? You didn't give me a chance," he said, not allowing her the opportunity to defend her actions. He managed to keep his voice low enough not to frighten the boy. "And why are you telling me now?"

Her face was as pale as the white T-shirt she wore over a pair of blue jeans. She swayed, and he caught her elbow.

He muttered a curse. "You okay, Kel?" he asked, surprised at how calm his voice sounded when anger still pounded in his ears.

"I'm a little tired is all." She stepped away from his touch, then looked from him to the child in her arms. "This is William James. He goes by Will." Her eyes turned soft and warm as they lingered on the boy.

He studied the child's chocolate-brown eyes, thick mahogany hair and olive complexion—too many similarities to ignore.

The boy watched him from the security of Kelly's arms. Their eyes met and held until the toddler lowered his head against Kelly's breast.

Something shifted in James's chest, flooding him with an intense need to protect and something else he wasn't sure he wanted to examine. "You should have told me before you left."

"I didn't know then." She stifled a yawn.

He caught Kelly's elbow and steered her to a chair, her arm fragile in his hand. "Let's sit down where we can talk, before you fall asleep on your feet."

Kelly sat on the edge of the chair. "I'm sorry. I've studied hard the past two weeks, even pulled several all-nighters. I loaded the truck yesterday after my last final and drove straight through from College Station to Willow Grove." She tried to hide another yawn behind her hand. "I'm really, really tired, but I had to tell you."

"Look, we've got some things we need to talk about, but you can barely keep your eyes open. Why don't we go to my place? You can sleep for a while, then we'll talk." It would give him some time to think this whole thing through. After he cooled off.

She stood and blinked several times, as if focusing

was difficult. "No, there's so much to explain, so much I need to say. Just let me go splash some cold water over my face."

He caught her arm when she tried to pass him. "Kel, I've already waited a couple of years. I reckon I can wait a while longer." Maybe by then he would have regained control of the old feelings that had suddenly resurfaced. It was almost as if she'd never left. Only, he knew she had.

And now he knew she had also betrayed him.

The child began to fuss, and Kelly kissed his brow. "Just a second, sweetie, and we'll leave." She gave James an apologetic smile. "There's a hotel not far from here where Will and I can get a room."

"There's no need for that," he said, wondering at her reluctance to go home with him. Maybe it made her feel uncomfortable to go back to the place where they'd made love. "Look, Kel, you don't need—"

"Thanks, but I can't impose on you and your, uh, roommate."

"Roommate?" Why would she think he had a roommate? He'd never had one before. "You care to explain that?"

When the child began to squirm, she shifted him to her other hip. "I assume you have someone living with you, James, that's all."

"Someone? You mean a woman?"

"No, James, I meant a tractor," she said, her lips turning up in a grin that wavered, then slipped away as her eyes settled on him. "Of course I mean a woman."

He had no intention of telling her he had only gone out twice since she'd left. Both times he had known five minutes into the date that it wouldn't work. Because neither of the women had possessed Kelly's quick wit or her sassy mouth. And neither had made him feel the way she did. "No, Kel, there's no one."

"Oh."

"So will you go home with me now?"

When she didn't answer right away, he said, "Come on. I'm not the big bad wolf. I'll behave."

Despite struggling to keep her eyes open, she smiled. "You forget I know you."

"Can't blame a fella for trying." He lifted the restless child from her arms. Funny how holding Will seemed almost natural. He chalked it up to holding Cal's daughter, Jessie, on more than one occasion. But this was different. This was *his* son.

He'd missed out on so much. As bad as he hated to admit it, he'd missed her while she'd been away at vet school. He'd missed the way she'd always pestered him, how she'd dragged stray cats and dogs to the clinic during off time and how she'd restored order to his disorderly life. But that was before she'd run out on him. Before this unthinkable deception.

James could see Kelly was exhausted. Her clothes hung on her as if she'd recently lost weight. She'd always pushed herself until she dropped, forgetting to eat, functioning on very little sleep.

As he led her outside, he circled his arm about her waist to steady her. She was so thin he could have spanned her waist with his hands. Half-asleep, she paused beside him while he locked the clinic door.

James noticed the slump of her shoulders, as if she bore the weight of the world—but then, Kelly always had. The sun low on the horizon revealed dark shadows beneath eyes that had once sparkled with life.

Lines of exhaustion bracketed lips that used to smile without effort.

Her keeping the child a secret angered him, but his immediate concern was her welfare, because, as usual, it looked as though she'd taken care of everyone except herself.

The struggling child in his arms proved there was a side to her he didn't know—a side capable of harboring painful secrets. For the time being he'd have to be content to know that by this time tomorrow he would have answers.

"Kel, you're not in any shape to drive. Get in and scoot over. I'll drive your truck and come back tomorrow to get mine."

She gave him a smile that slid into a yawn. "I see you're still as hardheaded as ever, James Scott, but I'm too tired to argue. You can drive, but take it easy. I've got Matilda in the horse trailer."

"You still hauling that broken-down nag around?"

"She's family." Kelly leaned against the pickup's fender. He hurried to steady her and lowered the boy to the ground, careful to see the child had his balance before he lifted Kelly and settled her inside the truck. When Will began to fuss, James picked him up and walked to the passenger's side where he strapped the toddler into his car seat. He found a cup with a top and a built-in straw in the seat and stuck it in his mouth.

James circled her truck and horse trailer. Both had been junkers five years ago when Kelly had first come to work for him and his partner, Cal, at the veterinary clinic. They still were.

After checking the trailer hitch, he opened the driver's door and paused. The end of Kelly's long braid hung over her shoulder. Wild tendrils of gold had escaped the uneven plait and danced in the warm May breeze carrying the smell of a nearby hay field through the open windows. His hands itched to smooth the strands back into place.

So many times he'd thought of her. He had set out more than once to find her, but each time had come back empty-handed. Now it was as if she'd never left. As if everything was the same.

Except for the child.

And the lie.

After moving a blue notebook from the seat to the floor, James eased her over to sit between him and the boy. Reaching across her, he hooked her seat belt. Awareness swirled around him, beckoning him with her sweetness. He set his jaw, determined to ignore the familiar scent imbedded in his mind. He needed to keep a clear head, something he'd never been able to do around her, until they hashed things out.

He put the truck in gear and eased out the clutch. As he pulled away from the clinic, his attention on the trailer behind him, Kelly slid closer to him, her head nuzzling his shoulder.

James glanced at her. "From the looks of you, it definitely would have been a mistake to let you drive."

"We made one mistake," she mumbled, more asleep than awake. "We can't afford to make another."

He wasn't sure whether she meant their one night together or the child. Either way, he wanted to argue the point with her, but she was already out.

He didn't understand how she could have kept news of her pregnancy from him. She had never been one to play games. The only person who had more rules than Kelly was his dad, and, like the sergeant major, she lived by every stinking one of them.

Considering that, he cursed under his breath and glanced around her to the boy. Though Kelly had passed out, he should have been the one to faint dead away, after learning he was the father of a two-year-old.

Will offered Kelly his cup. When she didn't move, the toddler cocked his head to one side and said, "Mama night-night."

Warmth spiraled through James. "Yeah, Will. Mama's gone night-night."

The kid nodded and caught the straw with his mouth, then settled back to watch James, wariness in his eyes, the same sort of uncertainty James now felt.

As he turned the pickup onto the county road leading to his land, he couldn't help but wonder if Kelly hadn't told him because she'd believed him irresponsible. A rush of anger accompanied that thought, and he tightened his hands on the steering wheel. Well, she'd made her last sole decision where Will was concerned.

From here on out, James would have a say in his son's future.

The bark of a dog somewhere outside drew Kelly from a deep sleep. She stretched and yawned, then turned on her side. The scent of potent male emanated from the pillow.

Kelly blinked several times before her eyes focused on framed photographs of horses against antique-white walls. A portable TV sat at an odd angle on the nightstand surrounded by stacks of veterinary medicine books and magazines.

She bolted into a sitting position and looked around. He had taken her to his bed. Again. Though last time she'd willingly followed him. Somehow she didn't remember the bed being so big…or lonely.

Even cloaked in darkness, with soft light slipping through the closed curtains, she recognized his bedroom. She'd memorized every detail during their one time together—the night his gentle touch and honeyed words had broken down her defenses. The night she had given in to the secret love she'd harbored for her best friend. The night she had turned her back on the principles that had been the only constant in her life for as long as she could remember.

Dogs barked again somewhere outside, and the sound of Will crying came through the closed door. Kelly's arms and legs felt heavy, but she yanked back the covers and jumped to her feet, thankful she still had on her clothes from the day before. Set into action by a deeply ingrained maternal instinct, she hurried to the door, wondering how long she had slept and whether Will was okay.

Her son's fussing grew louder as she dashed down the hall. She knew instinctively that the man she'd once idolized could handle a two-year-old. She'd watched James work on injured horses and knew he always exercised the utmost care and responsibility. But was James with Will? The need to see for herself that her son was unhurt spurred her forward. Heaven only knew what Will had gotten into while she'd slept. The possibilities made her stomach churn.

Pulse racing, Kelly skidded to a stop as she entered

the kitchen. Relief surged through her. She caught the door frame and drew a ragged breath.

Across the room her son knelt on a heavy oak chair pulled up to the open fridge. James stood beside him, dressed in jeans and a chambray shirt with cuffs rolled up to the elbow. Her gaze locked on his muscled forearms, then dropped to his standard, scuffed boots. She couldn't help but wonder if those were the same boots he hadn't managed to get off before they'd made love that first time. They hadn't gotten as far as his bed, either. At least not the first time.

Or the second.

She closed her eyes and tried to ground herself. She'd forgotten how his towering height, his mile-wide shoulders and his to-die-for smile had always affected her.

They still did.

But it was so much more than just the way he was put together and what he did for denim. Her feelings for him ran deep and extended beyond their one night of lovemaking. Her continued longing for him was fueled by the memory of his tenderness and the things he'd said. That she was beautiful. That he wanted her.

He had said things that almost made her forget she had spent most of her life feeling unwanted.

She opened her eyes as James pulled a cardboard box off a wire shelf and offered Will something shriveled and dried. "What about pizza?"

Kelly started to protest, but Will pushed the food away while fussing and jabbering unintelligibly. She recognized her son's renewed cries were caused by anger and frustration, probably from not getting his way. The only person more stubborn than Will was James. Again her thoughts whirled back to the night they had created Will. After the second time they'd made love, James had tried to tell her they needed to stop, because he didn't want to hurt her. Kelly smiled at the memory. She'd been shamelessly persistent. Afterward she had been glad she'd broken down his resistance. That one night was all she'd had with him. It was all she would ever have.

Muttering, James tossed the pizza box behind him onto the table, barely visible beneath a pile of discarded items—the same table where he'd made slow, mind-shattering love to her the first time. "You've already polished off the only soda I had. That leaves a six-pack of beer, and you can't have that."

Will slid to the floor and kicked. When he wanted something, he wanted it immediately.

"Yeah. No offense, partner, but you're a might young for beer."

Will sniffled and toddled over to James, catching the leg of his jeans at knee level.

Something in Kelly's chest shifted. She had known seeing James again would be difficult. But nothing had prepared her for the sight of father and son together. Regret filled her soul. She gulped a shaky breath before squaring her shoulders.

Kelly reminded herself that James had always been and probably still was a free spirit, not at all the commitment type. She would do well to remember why she'd left. But this wasn't about her.

Would James resent her for tying him down? Was he ready to raise a child, ready for that kind of commitment? These were the same questions she had asked herself when she'd made the decision not to tell him she was pregnant.

But there was no one else to raise Will should the need arise.

"All right, Will." James closed the refrigerator door and sat on the floor beside his son. "I reckon it's time to wake your mama."

Will crawled into James's lap, and the cowboy looked a little ill at ease as he held his son.

"I'm awake."

Will rushed at her, his bare feet slapping against the wood floor. She released the door frame and scooped him up into her arms. He snuggled against her shoulder, quiet and content for the moment. "Hey, sweetie. Have you been good?"

With his head buried in the curve of her neck, Will nodded.

Kelly sensed James watching her and tried not to look at him but failed. The cowboy still had the knack of disarming her with nothing more than a glance—and that glance had her remembering the rumpled bed they had fallen into the third time they'd made love.

As if reading her mind, James's heated gaze started at her feet and worked its way up, lingering here and there, making her pulse race and her temperature rise. His brown eyes darkened as they had that night—the night she had tried so hard to forget. But the memory of his unhurried touches and lingering kisses was forever seared in her mind.

Kelly stiffened. She didn't want to recall the gentleness of his callused hands, the way she'd responded to his touch, or the way his mouth had ignited flames that had consumed her.

No. She absolutely refused to think of that night again, but how could she forget when James kept looking at her like that?

"I—I'm sorry I couldn't stay awake," she said. "Thanks for watching Will."

James shrugged and pushed to his feet, his seductive eyes never leaving her. "After I shower, we'll head into town for some breakfast. I've had all night to think about us and what happened—"

"There is no *us,* James. There never was," she said, the lie bitter on her tongue. "It was just sex between consenting adults, that's all. And only the one night." Kelly was sickened by her deceit and tried to walk past him, but he blocked her path, his nearness making her heart pound. "If you'll excuse me, I need to get Matilda out of the trailer and feed her."

He touched her arm, then let his fingers trail down to her wrist, sending shock waves through her body. "We put her in the barn last night with my horses and went out earlier to feed the old nag. The boy seemed to get a kick out of that."

"Thanks," she said, cursing the wobble in her voice.

James watched her, his eyes clouding over like a summer storm. "I want answers, Kel. I don't think you can convince me that what you did was right, but I'm willing to listen...after I shower." James caught the front tails of his shirt and yanked. The snaps popped open, and as if drawn by a homing device, her gaze became riveted to his tanned chest and the dusting of dark hair.

"I'll hurry," he said as he strode past her and down the hall, his faded jeans caressing his backside with every fluid shift of his slender hips.

Her thoughts shattered. Kelly pulled a chair away from the table with a shaking hand and lowered herself, careful not to wake Will who had fallen asleep

in her arms. She had convinced herself she would be
immune to James's blatant sexuality. Grabbing an envelope off the table to use as a fan, Kelly admitted she
might have been wrong. Even though there were sub-
tle differences in him, she had done the right thing by
leaving. James was still too gorgeous for his own
good. He oozed more sex appeal than should be legal.
Still, he was Will's father.

She cringed, knowing she shouldn't blame everything on James. He couldn't help how he looked or
the way females threw themselves at him. She had
watched him trying to put them off without hurting
their feelings; he really was a good man. And living
with James would be a sight better than having Will
grow up in foster care with nothing but rejection and
loneliness as his companions—if something happened
to her.

She knew all about loneliness. It had sent her into
James's arms even though she'd seen him shy away
from commitment with other women. After he'd made
love to her, she had refused to cling to him the way
some had tried. Unwilling to watch him withdraw
emotionally from her, she had decided that for once
in her life *she* wouldn't be the one left behind and
hurting. So, she'd done the only thing she could do—
she'd left.

Kelly shifted Will on her lap and breathed in
James's scent that lingered on her son. Their son.

Odd she should be here now, seeking the aid of the
fun-loving man she'd tried so hard to forget, but he
was Will's father. And she had no one else to turn to.
Over her lifetime she'd made a lot of rules that she
observed diligently. Coming back, speaking to James,
meant breaking rules sixteen and seventeen, but there

had been no other way. She couldn't bear the thought of Will ending up alone. She wanted him to know James's love.

Even if she never would.

Chapter Two

"Why didn't you tell me?" James asked, leaning back in the café booth, the toes of his boots bumping against the other side. "I think I deserved to know."

The hurt and anger raging inside him was directed at himself as much as Kelly. Not long after she'd left, he had tried to find her. He'd known nothing about her family. Maybe if he'd bothered to ask more questions about her past he might have found her. Maybe if he'd hired a private investigator after his own attempts had failed he would have known about his son.

"I know I made some mistakes and in the process hurt you and Will," Kelly said, sounding defeated. "I can only say I struggled with my decision. I'm sorry, James, I never intended—"

"Sorry? Sorry is for forgetting to ask if I want onions on my hamburger. Sorry is for leaving the gate open and letting the mare out. But sorry doesn't cut it with something as life changing as forgetting to tell me I have a son.''

She flinched as she finished pouring syrup over the child's pancakes before placing the saucer on the highchair tray. ''You have every right to be angry with me.''

''You're damned right I do.''

''No matter what you think, I really did struggle with whether or not to tell you.''

''For two years, Kel?''

''I wasn't sure you would want to know.''

''What the hell does that mean?''

''Please don't raise your voice. It upsets Will.''

When several customers looked their way, he focused on his clenched hands and counted to five. He noticed the child's mouth quivered as if he might cry, but a comforting word from Kelly calmed him.

She met James's gaze, lifting her coffee mug, clutching it until her knuckles turned white. ''Not long after I returned to school, I began feeling awful. I got up sick and went to bed sick. I had to drop three classes to pull a decent grade in the others.''

''If you'd told me—''

''Please let me finish. I'm being honest with you and would like the same from you. If you *had* known, would you have come for me? Would you have married me and settled down?'' she asked, her eyes filled with a deep sadness that tore at his insides. ''And if you had done those things, would it have been because you wanted to or because you had to? And afterward would you have blamed me for ruining your life?''

He dragged a hand through his hair, not at all pleased with the conclusions she'd drawn, then and now. Maybe the only conclusions she could've drawn, considering his history with women. "Since you didn't bother to tell me you were pregnant with *my* child, you know I don't know what I would have done. But for that matter, neither do you."

Kelly met his gaze. "James, you are a wonderful friend. My best friend…at least you used to be. In spite of what you might believe, I thought about this a long time before making up my mind. I didn't think you would offer marriage, so I focused on Will."

"Tell me the truth, Kel. Did you even consider what I'd want?"

"Do you think you could have made a life-long commitment to Will? I don't mean dropping in once every year or so when you were passing through to a rodeo or hauling a horse to breed—but making planned trips to see him, only him. Being a father means making time, even if you miss your first ride at the next rodeo."

"Whether I could have done that isn't the issue here. You had no right to make that decision for me," he said, no longer caring if other customers overheard.

"I realized not long ago that I'd been wrong to not tell you," she said. "I can't undo what I did or give you back the lost time with Will, but I can give you his future. I'm here for the summer so you can get to know your son."

He wasn't sure he'd heard her right, couldn't figure out why she'd changed her mind. Until this moment blaming her had somewhat eased the stinging blow to his pride, but now the impact of her words hit him like the kick of a mare. Rather than rejoice that she had finally admitted to being wrong and was now allowing him to be Will's father, he wondered whether he really could be a father. A good father.

His relationship with his own father was dismal at best. His dad barked orders, pointed out every mistake and expected James to jump like his troops on the military base. He'd always claimed he did it to make James better, stronger.

In spite of their inability to agree on anything, James called his dad every couple of weeks. Their conversations always ended in an argument. His father would point out that a real man would want to defend his country. James resented the not-too-subtle reminder that his dad believed him an irresponsible failure.

He watched Kelly help Will get a drink of milk. The boy fussed when she wiped his mouth with a moist towelette, using hands that were gentle yet strong, like the woman.

He had missed her, the friendship they'd shared, the way she had always supported him, believed in him without question. And he didn't understand what had caused everything to get so messed up between them. "Kel, how can you have been so sure what I would have done back then, when I don't know the answer myself? And what's different now, that made you change your mind about me?"

Kelly tossed the used towelette on the table. "James, please."

She pulled the tray out from the high chair and lifted Will into her lap. "I struggled and struggled with this from the beginning, wanting to tell you, hoping that maybe if you knew..."

"What?"

She bit her bottom lip. "I wanted to do the right thing for all of us—you, me and our child. I must have picked up the phone a million times."

James frowned. He might have had a wild streak back then, but he wanted to think he would have taken care of his child. Sure, he'd always had to prove himself by riding the meanest bronc and the rankest bull, driving the fastest car and tossing back the most beer, but last year a bad spill in Fort Worth had made him realize he was jeopardizing his veterinary career. Now he only competed if someone needed a partner in team roping on weekends. Regardless, she ought to know he wasn't completely without values.

"You should have called," he said. "I would have come after you—"

"I did call."

"When?"

"After Will's birth." Kelly nestled her cheek against the child's head and cradled him in her arms, rocking back and forth as the boy's hand caught hold of her braid, which had fallen over her shoulder.

"I don't understand. I never got your message." James couldn't force himself to look away from their son playing with her hair. Memories of taking it down, running his hands through the thick mass and then, later, enjoying the feel of it across his chest distracted him.

"I didn't leave a message. When I called, some woman answered."

"A woman?"

"For all I knew, you had settled down with a live-in girlfriend or maybe even married. I didn't want to complicate things for you, so I hung up."

He frowned, trying to figure out who had answered his phone. "I've never had a woman living with me. When did you call?"

"May fifth at seven o'clock in the morning, two years ago."

Realization dawned. "That was my baby sister, Lindsey."

Kelly stilled. "Lindsey?"

"Yeah. She and her husband, Joe, and their two kids came for a visit. Joe had graduated from officer-candidate school at Fort Sill, Oklahoma, and been made into what we always called a 'shake and bake' officer. They stayed here a week, then made their way to Houston where they caught a flight to Germany for a four-year hitch in the Army."

"I didn't know. I assumed—"

"You were wrong."

She cocked her head to the side. "I see that now, but it was a natural assumption."

"How do you figure that?"

"James, you're like the blue-light special at the grocery. You can't blame me for believing that some woman shopping for a man had finally snapped you up."

"Why shouldn't I? You blamed me for something I didn't do." He didn't like how she made him feel, as if he were responsible for the man-chasing rodeo groupies. A niggling doubt sprang into his mind, and while he couldn't accept it, he found himself asking, "Is that why you stayed with me that night? To see if you could snap me up?"

Her eyes widened. "Do you really believe I'd do that just to see if I could succeed where others had failed?"

He shrugged, his shoulders stiff.

"If you have to ask, it means you don't know me at all," she said.

"That's the problem, Kel. I'm only now finding out I didn't know you at all."

Kelly shot him an exasperated look. "How can you say that?"

"Why did you do it, then? Were you using me to make someone else jealous?"

She stared at him a long time, and when he didn't think he could stand the pain in her eyes any longer, she whispered, "No."

Relief surged through him. He leaned his elbows on the table, admitting to himself that why she'd gone to his bed didn't really matter now. It was in the past. His personal history had taught him to let go of things he couldn't change, but he couldn't easily dismiss what she had done.

James took a drink of coffee and remembered something she'd said. "You mentioned the rodeo a while ago. I know you've never really cared much for that part of my life. Did that have anything to do—"

"No. I didn't used to like you to compete because of the risks you took. You could have been injured or worse."

He didn't plan to tell her an injury is what had made him quit. "I don't have time for much of anything except the clinic now."

"James, I know you're really mad at me, but I'd like you to do me a favor. I was talking about priorities and whether you'd be able to make a commitment to Will. I'd like you to think about that and then answer it. Not for me, but for yourself. Answer it truthfully. Regardless of what you think, I didn't come back to take potshots at you. Nothing would make me happier than to discover I'd misjudged you."

She was right. The admission was like a burr under

his saddle. She had based her decisions on what was best for Will, and he needed to do the same, but it was damned hard whenever Kelly was close at hand. He reacted to her nearness even while clinging to his hurt pride.

Her mentioning his need to avoid commitment opened old wounds he hadn't allowed himself to think about for years. Although hidden deep inside, they were still raw and hurting even after all this time.

James swallowed past the ache that threatened to choke him. "You were wrong about me, about everything. I can be a good father. In fact, I intend to prove it now."

James walked from the barn, still stinging from his conversation with Kelly earlier that morning. He heard the rattle of her truck as it bounced over the ruts in his drive. By the time he had made it to the front of the house, she was lifting Will from his car seat. "Did you find an apartment for the summer?" he called.

"Nothing I'd consider," Kelly said, pushing back several strands of hair that had worked loose from her braid and blown across her face. "Since I'm still paying rent to keep my apartment in College Station I can't afford much. There are plenty of cheap places if I want to live with roaches or rats. I'm kind of strange about sharing my living space."

He caught the diaper bag from the back of her truck and, ignoring Kelly's protests, lifted Will from her arms. "Here, let me help. You look as if you're about to fall down. You should have let me go with you."

She turned to look at him. "As you pointed out earlier, you have work to do, and I'm not helpless."

He noticed again the shadows beneath her eyes and

wished he'd kept his mouth shut about the chores he had to do. Yeah, he had a schedule to keep, but his refusal to accompany her had come more from the blow to his pride. He still couldn't believe she thought he would have turned his back on his son.

Knowing she hadn't needed him was hard to accept. But she had always been self-sufficient to the point of needing no one, something that used to bother him. It still did.

"Of all people you should know I don't think you're helpless, but little Will here is a chunk," he said. "I'm here now, so let me help."

"Okay," she said, turning away, but not before he saw the worry and something that resembled remorse in her eyes. He shouldn't want to comfort her, but he did. And that aggravated him almost as much as the realization that he hadn't known her the way he'd once thought he had. But then, she'd always been content to sit and listen to him. He doubted there was anything about him she didn't know. Only now did he realize she'd seldom talked about herself. The things he did know about her, he'd learned from years of observation.

"If I'm supposed to bond with Will, it makes sense for you both to stay here with me," he said. "After all, it's only for the summer."

That statement earned him a frown from her. He didn't care whether she liked it or not. He had every intention of spending time with his son, no matter what she wanted.

Kelly climbed the steps to his porch, her feet dragging. "You know I can't do that."

"Why?" James followed her, trying not to notice the gentle sway of her jean-clad hips. He opened the screen door and held it while she stepped inside, then cursed himself for watching her cross the room.

About the time sweat began to pop out on his forehead, she turned back to face him. "You don't need us underfoot all the time. You know I'd drive you crazy."

She had a point. She was driving him crazy now— he was insane with a need for her, a need to kiss that mouth.

He watched her, noticing she avoided looking him in the eye. "Bull. I tolerated you just fine before."

"That was at work. You're not used to having extra people around your house. I think it's best—"

"Best? For who? You?"

"For Will, of course. Everything I do is for him."

"I hope *you're* buying that lame excuse, Kel, because I'm sure not."

He knew why she didn't want to stay, and it had nothing at all to do with inconveniencing him. She obviously didn't think he'd be a good example for the boy. A sudden feeling of inadequacy filled him, replaced in an instant with anger that had been smoldering, barely under control, since that morning. "You're using all these convenient excuses same as when you made your decision not to tell me about Will."

His tone made Will pucker up to cry.

"Aw, hell," James muttered.

Kelly shot James a dirty look as she took Will and lifted him to her shoulder. She calmed the child with quiet words and loving pats on his back that distracted James.

When the boy had stopped crying, Kelly squared

off across from James. "What did you mean excuses?"

"Come off it, Kel. You know exactly what I meant. You think I'll have him chewing tobacco and chasing women by the time he's three." James kept his voice low, but didn't know how he'd managed it, because his insides churned.

Her eyes blazed as she stared at him. "I think I'd better leave. This isn't getting us anywhere. If it's all right with you, I'd like to keep Matilda here until I can find a place to board her. I've got some feed in the trailer, but will pay you—"

James tore his fingers through his hair. "Don't do this, Kel."

"I think we've proven we can't be in the same room without sparks flying. We both need to cool down. I've already done several things I swore not to do. I won't make an already difficult situation worse." She caught the strap of the diaper bag and lifted it over her shoulder.

"Where are you going?" James asked, knowing he shouldn't care. But he did.

"To get a room at a motel." She headed out the door toward her truck.

He wanted to stop her, pull her into his arms and hold her. It made no sense at all, but nothing ever had, not where Kelly was concerned. Swearing under his breath, he followed her. "Will you call and let me know where I can reach you?"

"I want to visit Cal and meet his new wife, so I'll drop by the clinic sometime tomorrow." She hooked Will in his car seat and hurried around the rusted-out truck.

Unable to watch her go, James strode after her and

caught the door just before she closed it. "Kel, wait. Can't we talk?"

She swallowed hard and looked out the windshield. "I don't know if that would help."

"I'm here now, willing to listen. What do you say we give it a try?"

"I'm too tired to talk today," she said.

"At least let me know what motel you're at." He finally let her slam the door.

With a lingering glance in his direction, Kelly started the pickup and backed down his driveway.

James stood there long after she'd disappeared around the curve in the road. He thought about all the things she'd said today and found he didn't much like what he'd heard or the way he saw himself through her eyes.

It had been a long time since James had felt this out of sorts. He shouldn't care about Kelly's plans for his son's future or that they didn't seem to include him; he hadn't even known about the boy until twenty-one hours ago. The fact that he worried about her at all irritated him almost as much as his inexplicable need to be with his son...and Kelly.

He headed toward his truck, cursing the vision of her that suddenly filled his head. Maybe several beers would help him forget how good she looked and her enticing scent. He doubted it would.

He needed to forget that while struggling to bring his child into this world, Kelly had found suffering alone preferable to leaning on him.

Kelly locked the motel door and slid the chain in place. She didn't like the room or the location of the motel, but after stopping at five others that were full because of the rodeo in town that weekend, she would have to make do. Her only other option was to stay with James. She didn't know if she could do that without slipping up and letting him see how much she still cared.

"Here, sweetheart, let me get your horse." She pulled the stuffed horse from the diaper bag and gave it to Will, who settled on the floor with his favorite toy.

The room echoed with loneliness after the time she'd spent with James. Funny, she'd lived alone until Will's birth, then it had been just the two of them. After only one day with James, she realized how much she'd missed adult conversation—almost as much as she'd missed him. Sure, she'd been around other students, but they were always listening to lectures. After class, she'd rushed to her job. And then there'd been Will.

Kelly's thoughts drifted back to James. She had wanted to stay with him, but no telling what she would have done if she had. That's why she'd created rule fifteen, to prevent that from happening. Though, actually, he had surprised her. He hadn't done any of the things she'd expected when he'd learned he had a son. With only minimal ranting and raving, he'd taken her home with him, and even after she'd made a mess of explaining things by blurting out her feelings, he'd offered them a room.

She wasn't sure the cowboy she'd once known would have sat still while she questioned his character. And if he had, he certainly wouldn't have asked her to stay.

And now, thinking back on all she'd said, Kelly couldn't remember when she'd wanted anything more than to be with James. Her reasons for leaving had everything to do with the way James had made her feel, just as it had before she'd left town three years ago.

Seeing him again had been a shock. The hurt she'd glimpsed when he'd thought she was married had almost been her undoing. But she'd prepared herself, knowing being around him again after all this time would be difficult. She'd formulated several new rules especially for the occasion. Still, it had taken all her strength to keep from walking into his arms, the only place she wanted to be.

Maybe she should call him. After all, he had asked how he could locate her. What could it hurt? She could smooth things over, make sure he hadn't taken offense to her refusal to stay with him. If he got angry, he might change his mind about getting to know Will, and that's why she'd put them both through the hell of telling him he had a son.

Kelly sat on the edge of the bed and punched in James's home phone number. She knew it by heart, having dialed it hundreds of times in the past. Kelly clutched the phone so tightly her hand ached. After the sixth ring she replaced the receiver on the cradle as she had so many times before.

She stood and paced the room, so tired she wanted nothing more than to go to bed. What if he had gotten upset? What if he'd had an accident? What if he had gone out with another woman? Kelly patted Will's head as she hurried back to the phone, her pulse racing as she dialed James's cell phone number.

He answered on the fourth ring. "It's your nickel."

The twang of country music drifted through the phone line, all but drowning out his voice.

She started to hang up, thinking that he might actually be with someone else. One glance at Will made her change her mind. "James?"

"Kelly?"

She imagined him seated in some honky-tonk with a voluptuous blonde on each knee. "I—I wanted to let you know where I'm staying, in case you need me."

"Just a sec." The crackle of paper sounded. "Okay, shoot."

"I'm at the Country Inn."

"What room?"

Kelly paused, trying to decide whether to tell him. What could it hurt? If an emergency arose, he would need to know how to contact her. Besides, she'd missed him and their friendship and hoped they could regain the easy camaraderie they'd always shared, though secretly she would always want more. If his friendship was all she could have, then that was better than nothing. Nothing is what she'd had the past three years. She'd missed him more than she'd believed possible. There were worse things than being just his friend.

"Kelly, are you still there?"

"Yeah. It's room twenty-two."

"Have you had supper?" he asked, his voice a seductive rumble that sent a shiver of awareness through her.

"No, I thought once we got settled maybe we'd get something."

"Would you let me take you and Will out to eat?"

Her pulse sped up. She wanted to say yes, but feared it would be a repeat of their earlier conversation. "I'm really tired, and tomorrow will be another full day of looking for a place to live.''

''What if I grab some burgers and swing by?''

Kelly knew she should refuse, but she really was more exhausted than she'd thought. ''I'd like that, James. But could you bring a grilled cheese sandwich for Will?''

He didn't respond for a moment, and if it hadn't been for the music blaring over the phone line, she would have thought they'd lost their connection. Finally he said, ''Great. I'll be there in fifteen minutes.''

''All right,'' she said, the words coming out thick, sounding like someone else. The connection went dead then, and Kelly listened to the buzz for a minute before returning the phone to its cradle.

Inviting James to her room had been foolhardy. She knew better. The knowledge that he would be there shortly sent an adrenaline rush through her. But she had a responsibility to her son. She'd made a promise to him and to herself, a promise she intended to keep. She wasn't about to let an excess of hormones and one sexy cowboy get in the way of her child's future.

When James arrived, she would take the food, thank him for his trouble and ignore him while he visited with Will. She had fallen for James's good looks once. No, that wasn't necessarily true. It had been so much more than just his looks, and she reminded herself of why she'd come back.

Kelly had only invited James over because she was too tired to go and get Will's dinner. Anyone could make a mistake…once. From now on, she would stay focused on her goal. She would not fail. Her son's future depended on it.

As of this minute James Scott could walk naked into

the room and she would not notice. It was a simple matter of discipline and concentration.

Of course, she'd never been able to hold a thought around him.

With or without his clothes.

Chapter Three

James parked in front of room twenty-two of the Country Inn and shut off his truck. He opened his door, grabbed the sack of food and tray of drinks and slid from the pickup, kicking the door shut.

Two disreputable-looking thugs sat on the hood of a car a few rooms down. Another three straddled motorcycles. They watched James, their body language challenging and belligerent, something he knew about firsthand. Without turning his back on them, he knocked on the door. After the way things had gone earlier with Kelly, he would welcome a good fight, but first he needed to make sure she and Will were safe.

When the lock turned and the door swung open, he stepped inside without waiting for an invitation. "Pack your bags."

Kelly's mouth fell open, and she sputtered.

"Do you have any idea of the lowlifes that roam this area?" he asked. "There are five waiting outside right now, probably planning what they'll do to you when I leave. You can forget staying here."

He knew she'd gone from shock to anger when her mouth pursed and her eyes turned cold as the pond in his south pasture in January. And he didn't think her spine could get any more rigid.

"In case you didn't notice, James, there is a lock on the door and a safety chain."

"Yes, and those guys out there can probably pick it faster than you can open it from the inside. In fact, they'd probably kick it in to save time. And that stupid chain is more for your peace of mind than protection. One good shove from the other side, and it'll pop."

A tug on one leg of his jeans made him look down. Will stood reaching for him. He bent to gather his son in his arms. It felt so strange, this intense need to protect.

Picking up Will had been as natural as drawing a breath. The boy leaned his head on James's shoulder, then seemed content to play with the snaps on his shirt.

Trying to sort through the things Will made him feel, James glanced around the shabby room, then turned to Kelly. "Get your stuff together. We're leaving."

She paced the length of the room, then turned back to him. "With the rodeo in town, there aren't any other rooms."

"Then you're staying with me."

At the uncertainty in Kelly's eyes, he stepped toward her. "I promise not to crawl into your bed when you go to sleep if that's what you're thinking."

She lifted her chin a fraction. "No, that's not what I thought."

"Good, because if you insist on staying here, then

I'm staying, too. And frankly I'm not sure that bed is big enough for the three of us—but I'm willing to give it a try.''

"I guess under the circumstances it wouldn't hurt to stay with you, just for one night," she said, unable to hide the worry in her voice. "Hopefully, I'll find a place of my own tomorrow."

It annoyed him that she seemed determined to put as much space as possible between them. "Like you said, Kel, this is about what's best for the boy."

She finally nodded as she covered a yawn. "I'll get our things."

When she'd packed their bags, James carried them out to his truck, then made sure she and Will were securely locked in her pickup without incident before he climbed into his. The five men were still seated outside the motel but were busy talking with a couple of women who had arrived.

When Kelly parked at the motel office to turn in the key, James pulled up beside her and told her to stay put. Ignoring her frown, he took the key and tossed it to the night clerk.

Once inside his truck, James signaled for Kelly to go on ahead. He didn't like the idea of her being out alone at night and intended to keep her in sight until they reached his place.

James was pleased Kelly hadn't put up much of an argument over staying with him. She sure hadn't much liked the thought of him sharing her motel bed. He probably shouldn't have said that. Not that it mattered. She already had a low opinion of him. In fact, it probably couldn't get much worse. For some reason that bothered him.

But he wouldn't dwell on that. He chose to recall

the warmth that had spread through him earlier when his son had lifted his arms, wanting James to hold him.

His son.

Kelly rolled the blanket James had tossed her and tucked it into the crack between the bed and the wall. "I hate to take your bed again, James. I don't mind sleeping on the couch."

"No. I stayed awake most of last night, trying to keep Will from rolling off that couch. It's best to put him in here with you. I'll sleep out there until I can get the spare bedroom cleaned out."

Despite his words, Kelly knew James's legs would hang over the edge of the couch. He wouldn't get any rest. Still, she knew it was better for her and Will to be in the bed. Used to a baby bed, her son twisted, turned, and flopped in all directions while he slept. Even with her on the outside as a barrier, she'd be lucky to keep Will from falling out during the night.

James lifted Will from the temporary pallet they'd made for him on the floor. Leaning across the bed on one knee, he settled the child on the far side.

Kelly rolled another blanket and put it down the center of the bed to keep Will from traveling too far.

"Well, I'll see you in the morning," James said as he headed toward the door. He paused and turned back to her. "I didn't mean to bully you, but I couldn't leave you at that motel."

She knew he had done the right thing. "I hadn't realized that area of town had run down so much since I'd left. I wouldn't have checked in if I'd known."

James didn't move to leave. He hooked a thumb in a belt loop and watched her watching him.

His day-old growth of whiskers lent him a sexy

look. He wore it well. "James," Kelly said, her voice husky, "you never asked me about Will, you know, whether or not he was yours."

A sadness she didn't understand filled his eyes. "You want me to ask for proof that he's mine?"

Actually, she wished he would shout, demand proof. Maybe that way she wouldn't feel so bad about not telling him. "I thought you would."

"I was your first, Kel. I don't deny that." His gaze moved over her, burning her with its intensity. "Of course, we only spent that one night together. And I was careful. I used protection every time."

"That's what I thought, but as you can see—" she inclined her head toward their child "—something went wrong. I don't remember you stopping to read the directions. Maybe you put them on wrong."

James laughed. "Me? Come on, Kelly, I'm not some snot-nose kid. I've used my share of condoms. I know what to do without reading the back of the box."

"And I've only been with one man. Ever." Now why the devil had she told him that?

Her admission brought a lazy smile to his lips, making Kelly wish she could take back the words.

"Why did you run out on me, Kel?"

She could hear the hurt in his voice, but knew well enough from her youth that people often forgot promises when it was convenient. She knew the pain of waiting for someone who never returned. At some point she'd quit believing anyone ever would.

After their one night together, she couldn't stand by not knowing whether he, too, would withdraw from her emotionally. Past experience had forced her to leave, so she wouldn't have to face him pulling away.

But she couldn't tell him that now. He wouldn't understand; she wasn't sure she did, either. Not anymore. Not after missing him so much.

She shrugged. "I had to get back to school."

James shifted his weight to the other hip, drawing her attention to the soft jeans molded to his powerful thighs and the shirt stretched tight across his broad shoulders.

His amber eyes beckoned, darkening until she could no longer distinguish his pupils from the irises. Time had deepened the creases that fanned outward from his eyes and set off an avalanche of memories of the last time they'd shared this room, that night after he'd won the rodeo.

They hadn't talked. They had communicated with tender caresses that made her burn, heated kisses that left her breathless and an insatiable need for each other that had kept them from sleeping until dawn.

Then she'd awakened. Alone. Even after learning he'd had an early clinic appointment, she couldn't shake her growing fear of abandonment.

She suddenly was almost too weary to stand. "If there's nothing else you want to know, I'd better get some sleep."

He studied the toe of his boot a minute, then crossed the room in three steps and paused much too close. Kelly backed up but hit the side of the bed.

James lifted a hand and ran the backs of his fingers down her cheek. "I'm sorry you went through having Will alone."

"It's over and done." She tried to ignore the blossom of heat that unfurled low in her belly at his touch.

His gaze lingered on her mouth.

Kelly licked her lips, trying her best not to notice

his scent or remember all the nights she'd lain awake thinking of him.

His fingertips pushed a strand of hair behind her ear, sending a tremor down her spine.

She locked her knees to keep from falling. "Good night, James."

He caught her nape.

Kelly gasped as he leaned toward her. His lips grazed hers. Once. Twice. Then they settled with firm possession on her mouth. So many times since leaving she'd wanted this kiss. And now, it was happening. Without thought of the consequences, she wound her arms around his neck and leaned into him.

She parted her lips and accepted what he would give, the steady heat of his mouth, the sweep of his tongue, the brush of his hand beneath her breast. The beating of his heart became one with hers as she tilted her head and deepened the kiss, her tongue dueling with his, taunting and teasing, wanting and needing still more.

James broke the kiss and tugged her arms loose, then stood there, chest heaving, and gave her a searching look. "Good night, Kel. Sleep tight." He turned and left the room, closing the door behind him.

Her legs gave out. She landed on the edge of the bed, her passion turning swiftly to anger. Darn it all. He had kissed her. And she had kissed him back.

So much for rule seventeen.

Kelly grabbed for something to steady herself as James steered her truck around yet another sharp bend in the road. Jammed between her son's car seat and James's wide shoulders, she gripped his muscled thigh. "We're not in a race, James. Would you slow down a little?"

"I thought you were wanting to speed things up a bit." He glanced down at the hand that had grabbed his leg and flashed her one of his race-you-to-the-bedroom smiles.

"Forget it," Kelly said with a teasing grin as she moved her hand away. "We're just friends, remember?"

"Last night you sure didn't kiss me like any friend I know."

Kelly swiped her hand across her forehead. "Whew! I'm glad to know that. I'd hate to see you kiss Cal that way when we get to his house."

"Very funny."

"Besides, that wasn't a kiss. I thought we were practicing CPR."

"Okay," James said. "I'll go along with that if it makes you feel better."

Just the mention of that kiss sent a rush of heat to her cheeks. Kelly tried to still her galloping heart. Touching him was like a cleansing by fire, but it came with a high price, a price she couldn't afford to pay. Especially now. Not when every decision affected Will. She would have to learn to ignore his finer points.

She lowered her eyes to the front of his chambray shirt he'd left unsnapped all the way down. The warm summer breeze ruffled the edges, exposing his tanned chest and the dark hair that narrowed before disappearing beneath the waistband of his jeans. Her gaze settled on his big...buckle.

Kelly swallowed hard and looked out the window. Not so long ago she'd run her hands across the corded strength of his shoulders. She knew precisely how all that lean muscle would feel beneath her fingers.

Two minutes, and she couldn't keep her eyes off him.

James secured his Resistol lower on his brow against the wind coming through the window. "What plans do you have for the summer?"

"None, actually, at least not now. The last couple of years, I've carried a killer schedule at school, taken care of Will after he was born, and worked part-time. I'm exhausted, physically and mentally. I decided not to take any summer classes."

"Sounds like you need a break."

"I hope to get a job that's not too demanding, that pays enough money to get us by."

Pulling up in front of Cal's house, James shut off the motor. "I'll help you with Will so you can catch up on your rest. You look worn-out."

"Thanks." She hoped it was only exhaustion, but that niggling feeling kept rearing up that maybe it was more. She needed to find out, but was afraid.

He climbed from the truck, snapping the front of his shirt as he went, and held the door for her as she scooted across the bench seat.

She slid out, taking the hand he offered. Warmth spiraled through her at his touch, and she would have been content to stay there the rest of the day.

When Cal's collie, Shep, rushed out to greet them, James bent down to pet the dog, but it swerved around him to jump on Kelly. She hugged Shep, who did his best to wash her face as she scratched him behind his ears. Kelly laughed when she saw James's scowl. "I can't believe he remembers me."

"You're not exactly easy to forget," he said.

Kelly's heart skipped a beat. What had he meant by that? Probably nothing. She was overly sensitive after that darned good night kiss, looking for things, hoping to see things that hadn't been there before and wouldn't be there now. It was plain foolishness the way she let him get to her. She had made a mistake by falling in love with her best friend. Now he was lost to her forever. At least she had her precious child. Still, if there was any chance of them regaining their friendship, she needed to ignore the way he made her feel. Not likely.

Still, their being friends was best for Will.

"You want me to get Will out?" he asked.

"No, thanks. I'll get him."

James walked toward the porch.

The front door banged shut, and James's partner, Cal, appeared, followed by a pretty woman who held a little girl about thirteen months old.

James paused, then turned back to Kelly. "Kelly, you already know Cal."

"Good to see you again," Cal said.

"This is Sara, his wife, and Jessie is their daughter."

Sara smiled. "You're just in time for breakfast," she said, settling the baby on one hip. "Hattie just started another pot of coffee."

"Let me get Will, and I'll take you up on the coffee," Kelly said, giving Shep one last hug. As she circled the truck, she noticed Jessie leaning toward James with her arms outstretched. As if that wasn't surprising enough, he took her.

"How's my girl been?" James asked, kissing the baby's chubby cheek.

Shock swept over Kelly, and her steps faltered. Finally she shut her gaping mouth and continued around the pickup. Before her return, she would have found James's actions as out of character as him wearing a suit and tie. But not now. Not with Will and now Jessie.

She stored the thought away and opened the truck door to unhook Will from his car seat. The question she'd already asked herself a hundred times since her return echoed once more in her mind. Had she been wrong about James? She rubbed her throbbing temples. No matter what the cowboy might seem to be now, at one time he had shied away from commitment.

Lifting her son, Kelly kissed the dark hair that was a shade lighter than James's and grabbed Will's diaper bag before starting toward the porch. She watched James with the little girl, his actions making it clear that holding Jessie was something he enjoyed and did often.

Kelly glanced away, unable to look at James cradling the child in his arms. So many times she'd wondered what it would have been like if they'd married. She had tried to imagine how it would be to see James with their son. Now she knew.

Needing to get away from the disturbing scene, Kelly hurried up the porch steps.

"Oh, yeah," James said, "the boy Kelly's holding is my son, Will."

Cal's mouth dropped open, and Sara's eyes grew wide.

Accepting their congratulations, Kelly followed Sara inside, but the sense of foreboding that crept through her remained.

The slight changes she'd noticed in James must

have been recent occurrences, resulting from his contact with Sara's and Cal's baby.

The only other possibility was that Kelly had been wrong about him all along. But that simply wasn't possible. Was it?

"What would you think about Kelly working for us this summer?" James asked Cal, once the front door shut behind the women.

"How do *you* feel about that?" Cal asked. "I know before she left here you two seemed to have gotten pretty close. And considering what you just dropped on us about the boy, obviously I was right."

James placed a supportive hand on Jessie's back as the child stared up at him. "I'm okay with it. She mentioned needing a job and since she's worked here before, I thought…"

"What about you, where do you figure in her plans?"

"I don't know. Maybe not at all, but she's here for the summer. She hasn't had an easy time of it. I'd like to do what I can to help."

"What about the boy?" Cal asked. "Why didn't you tell us about him before now?"

"Because I didn't know about him until two days ago." James couldn't stop the regret that churned inside him. "I've got a lot of lost time to make up for."

"With the boy or Kelly?" Cal asked, turning toward the house. He opened the door, then paused. "You two have a son. Sometimes doing the right thing isn't easy."

"What do you mean by that?"

"Just think about the boy before you decide anything. Come on. Hattie's probably got breakfast on the table.''

James followed his friend inside, wondering what in blue blazes Cal was trying to get at, but couldn't ask as Sara strode forward to get Jessie.

Cal's housekeeper, Hattie, patted James as he walked past to hang his hat on a peg by the back door before making his way to his usual place at the table. ''Looking at that boy over there is like seeing a miniature of you,'' Hattie said.

Pride filled him. He sat down and smiled at Kelly.

Hattie placed a platter of food in front of him and ushered Kelly to the chair on his right. Cal and Sara claimed the chairs directly across the round table.

James spread butter and grape jelly on a biscuit. He paused to watch Will, who had a choke hold on a spoon with his left hand and pushed a hunk of egg around his plate with the index finger of his right.

James offered the biscuit to Will, who took it without hesitation. A heaviness centered in his chest. He'd missed Will's first steps, his first words, and other firsts he couldn't begin to know about, but most of all, he hated that for two years he'd been a stranger to his own son. So much time to make up.

''James, I was telling Kelly the old Martin place is for rent,'' Sara said as she placed Jessie in a high chair. ''She wants to go take a look after breakfast. It's empty. She could move right in.''

''The hell she will,'' James said around a mouthful of biscuit. He knew Kelly wouldn't like it. She'd made all the decisions about Will since his birth, but that had been before James had learned he had a son.

Kelly's fork stilled halfway to her mouth. ''Excuse me?''

Cal gave James a warning look from across the table.

James glanced at Kelly. "You're not renting a house. You and Will are staying with me."

Her chin lifted a fraction. "We talked about this, James."

"Oh, dear," Sara said. "I seem to have said the wrong thing."

Ignoring everyone but Kelly, James held her gaze with his. "No, we didn't discuss it. You told me what you planned. How am I supposed to bond with Will if you're living clear across town?"

Kelly settled the fork on her plate. She wiped her fingers on a napkin and moved a plastic container with a funny top closer to Will. "I don't want to impose."

"Listen, Kel, I talked to Cal. We'd like to offer you work at the clinic for however long you're here."

She looked from him to Cal and back. "Thank you. I appreciate it. I'll be able to apply the hours to what I need to qualify for prevet. I'll need to find someone to watch Will."

"I can help some," Sara said, "but, well, we're expecting another baby, and I've been pretty tired."

"Hey, congratulations, you two," James said, pleased for his friends. He'd never known two happier people, though Cal had damned near lost Sara before he'd come to his senses.

Cal grinned and gave Sara a hug.

"Congratulations," Kelly said.

Hattie snorted. "Heck, I've known it for weeks, probably before Sara even suspected."

Sara smiled. "What about putting Will in day care? There's a really great one in town."

Kelly lifted her coffee cup and drank. "I hate the thought of leaving him, but I know I have to."

"It's doable," James said. "You can stay with me. There's plenty of room. Then I can help you with him."

"No way. I'm not moving in with you."

"Why not?" James asked with a sideways glance at her.

"Well, it's not a good idea," she said.

His patience was stretched thin. "If you're worried living with me will compromise your good name, I'd say it's too late for that."

Cal and Sara exchanged a look.

Hattie, elbow deep in dishwater, pretended not to listen.

Kelly stood and tossed her napkin on the table. "You know I've never cared one way or another what other people thought."

"Good, then it's settled."

"No, it's not. My concern is for Will. Children need routines and familiar things. This move has been hard on him. I don't want to make it worse by changing everything. I'll only have to shift it again in the fall when we go back to College Station."

"The day care will be a new place. If you find an apartment, he's going to have to get used to that, too. Why can't he get used to my house? Everything is an adjustment, and you're just making excuses."

She opened her mouth to respond.

James bolted from his chair and braced his hands on the table. "You kept me from being there for Will's birth. I never got to hold him, feed him or walk the floor at night."

Tension stretched taut between them.

"Don't make me out to be the villain here," Kelly said, her hands fisted. "I've tried to do what's right."

"What's right for you or for Will?"

When Will stood in his chair, James picked him up and held him close, inhaling the sweet smell of little boy and grape jelly. Dark eyes so like his own stared back at James. He personally knew the confusion, hurt and eventual bitterness Will would confront in the coming years if Kelly had her way.

"Your days of making all the decisions for Will are over. And if you think I'll sit still while you try to take him from me again, then you're wrong about that, too."

Kelly paled. "What do you mean *try?*"

Kelly might not need him, but his child did. And he had no intention of letting him down. "Nothing will ever again keep me from my son. Nothing."

Chapter Four

Kelly reeled from James's threat and glanced across the kitchen table at Cal and Sara, who looked away as if embarrassed. She'd hoped he would want his son, but not permanently, unless the worst happened to her. "Surely you don't think you're going to stop me from moving to A&M to go to school? I'm doing it for Will."

James raked his free hand through his hair while holding Will on his hip with the other. "Dammit, Kel, he's my son, too. Don't I have any rights?"

Will fingered the pearl button on the pocket of James's blue chambray shirt, seemingly undisturbed by their argument.

She sighed, knowing James would take good care of his son. "Yes, you have some rights. I know you probably think I'm trying to punish you for what happened between us, but I'm not."

Cal pushed his chair back and stood, pulling Sara to her feet. "Listen, Sara and I need to go check a window in the back of the house." He lifted his daughter from the high chair and they started from the kitchen. Cal turned back. "Hattie, we'll need your help, too."

Hattie dried her hands. "You don't need my help. You just don't want me to hear anything—like I've ever been known to spread gossip."

After they had all left the room, James lowered Will to the floor, then crossed his arms over his chest. "It seems to me you're skirting the real issues. You stole two years of my son's life from me. You say you want me to be involved in his life now, but you're doing everything possible to keep us apart. So what I want to know is why did you really come back?"

Kelly didn't think she'd ever seen him this mad. Still, he hadn't really raised his voice, but the force behind his words left little doubt of his feelings. Well, he wasn't the only one hurt, and nothing he said now could ever undo the pain of her having to leave. "Think whatever you like, James. I've already explained why I returned."

He rubbed the back of his neck. "No matter what you think, I do care, and I want to spend time with my son. But you keep throwing up roadblocks."

Kelly dropped in her chair. She noticed James hadn't mentioned wanting to be with her. She hated the disappointment filling her soul to overflowing. Still, he was right. It had never occurred to her that he might want a permanent future with his son. She hadn't thought beyond a contingency plan in case something happened to her like it had to the man who'd been the closest thing to a father she'd known. Now she felt an unreasonable fear, almost as if James intended to take her son from her.

She obviously hadn't thought things through. If she had, she might have anticipated his demands. But the fact is she'd tried not to think of James at all. It had hurt way too much.

It still did.

A lock of dark-brown hair had fallen onto his forehead. She checked the urge to smooth it back into place. "I admit I assumed you wouldn't want to be involved in Will's raising."

He leaned across the kitchen table. "Well, you assumed wrong. You would've known that, if you'd told me about him. What did you plan to tell the boy later on when he asked about his dad?"

What had she planned to tell him? She'd thought about it over and over. "Since he's only two years old, I haven't had to worry about that yet." That wasn't technically correct. She had worried about that question hundreds of times, but had never come up with an answer she could live with.

"Come on, Kel. I've had a son out there I knew nothing about. I can't change the past, but now that I know about Will, I want to help, be a part of his life, only you're trying to keep me on the outside, looking in. I've missed too much already. I won't let you cut me out. I want to be there for *my* son."

"I...I didn't think you'd want him," Kelly said, lifting Will from the floor. She needed to hold her son, to regain her footing. "I'm sorry. I may have been wrong, but I did what I thought best at the time."

The intensity of the hurt in James's eyes burned her. "You never gave me a chance to decide for myself."

"I came back so you can get to know Will."

"Then let me do it." James sighed. "Come on,

Kelly. Accept our offer to work at the clinic, and stay with me.''

"I'd really rather work at the clinic than flip burgers.''

James's coffee cup stilled halfway to his mouth. His probing gaze locked on Kelly. "Then do it, and you and Will can stay with me.''

She removed Will's bib and wiped his face. "I don't know.''

"Come on, Kelly.'' James settled his cup on the table and pushed away, his look pinning Kelly in her chair. "I'm offering you a job and a place to live. You need to do a little bending. Or is it that you don't want to be around me?''

When she didn't answer, he crossed the room, grabbed his hat off the peg at the back door and marched outside.

The force of the door slamming behind James made Kelly flinch. She turned when she heard footsteps.

Cal entered the kitchen alone.

"You heard?'' she asked him.

"It was hard not to hear, the way you two were yelling.'' Concern etched Cal's face. "He's a good man, Kelly.''

"Yes, I know he is.''

"I think you owe it to that little boy there to give James a chance to prove what he's capable of.''

Kelly's throat tightened. "I don't know. This is harder than I'd thought it would be.''

Sara came up behind Cal and sat Jessie on the floor. "The right woman could make James settle down. I'm not saying it would be easy, but it can be done. I know. It's how I came to be married to Cal. Cowboys are a tough breed, Kelly. It's hard to get close to them.

They won't always let you see what's inside of them.
I've been around James enough to know he's hurting.''

Surprised at Sara's comment, Kelly didn't answer.
She hoped they would let it drop. She didn't like the
weight of guilt that made her shoulders slump.

They wanted her to give James another chance,
opening her heart up once more. Because of his free
spirit she'd never believed he was the settling down
kind. It had taken two years to get over her first en-
counter with the handsome cowboy.

Not that she'd ever really gotten over him.

She shouldn't let past rejections affect her decision.
James deserved to get to know his son. Living with
James would give them quality time before she re-
turned to school.

Kelly stood, not sure she could handle much more.
''I've changed my mind about looking at that house.''

Sara smiled. ''I'm glad. Cal and I will watch Will
while you go tell James.''

Kelly moved into the living room and caught a
glimpse of James out in the corral with a sorrel mare.
When he leaned down to check a hoof, the horse nosed
his shoulder. Then he rubbed the mare's withers and
walked toward the barn.

Had she misjudged him? Had she caused her own
unhappiness? She squeezed her eyes shut, unable to
watch him without remembering the heat of his touch,
the feel of his lips on hers. Even after all she'd been
through with the free-spirited cowboy, she knew the
pain of missing him and longed to feel his touch and
the strength of his arms again.

But she couldn't, not if they were to remain strictly
friends.

Because, if and when James promised to love and care for Will, should something happen to her, she had to know for certain that his vow came out of love for his son.

And not from any misguided or honorable sense of obligation to her.

James tightened the bandage around the quarter horse's foreleg, satisfied it was healing properly. He had taken a huge chance, using the method of treatment selected, but he'd believed the risk would pay off in the long run. At the sound of footsteps, he glanced up.

Kelly stood in the doorway, silhouetted in the midday sunlight spilling into the barn through the open double doors. She wrung her hands. Then, as if noticing the telling action, jammed them into the back pockets of her jeans. She took several tentative steps into the stall where he knelt. "We'll stay with you, James, if the invitation is still open."

He couldn't believe she'd accepted his offer—not after he'd kissed her last night and lost his temper this morning. James hadn't intended to kiss her. Hell, it had been the last thing he knew he should do, but the sight of her in the dim light of his bedroom had stolen whatever common sense he might have had.

The fact she'd responded to his kiss at all actually surprised him. That she'd finally become soft and compliant in his arms and leaned into him had made leaving her almost impossible. Afterward, he'd lain awake most of the night with a raging need, thinking about her, cursing himself to hell and back for wanting her.

The same thing he'd done after she'd left.

And now she'd come back, wanting to be friends again.

James pushed himself to his feet and wiped his hands on the legs of his jeans. He shouldn't want to be near Kelly again, shouldn't burn with a need to touch her after the way she'd kept his son from him, but he did.

He stood, allowing his gaze to leisurely follow the curves he knew lay hidden beneath her loose shirt and jeans…once, twice. "Offer's still good."

"Thanks." Her thick blond braid swayed at her hips, the sunlight illuminating the golden strands. Dust motes swirled around the stray hairs that had come loose. She moved into the stall, keeping to the other side of the horse, using it as a barrier between them.

Her intoxicating scent carried to James. Her sweetness filled his lungs, filled the emptiness he'd felt since her leaving. His body's reaction was immediate and powerful, but he tamped it down; there were still too many unanswered questions between them.

His sudden and forceful need to protect had surprised James. He'd always been a loner, never wanted any woman hanging around for more than a couple of hours. Until Kelly.

He frowned, not willing to consider his reaction to her. "I really do want to help you, Kel. If you need anything, anything at all, ask me. No matter what you think, I want what's best for Will. And you."

Kelly stroked the horse's neck. "I know you're still mad about the past and everything—"

"I'm not keeping score, Kel." He ran his hand down the horse's mane, his fingertips touching Kelly's hand. As their eyes met, he caught her fingers, giving in to the aching need to touch her. His thumb brushed back and forth over her knuckles.

She shivered, then tugged her hand from his and lifted her chin, eyes flashing. "You think I'm keeping score?"

James's attention was drawn to her mouth. It seemed to beg for his kiss. "Yeah. You're clutching every mistake I've ever made like Shep holds on to a steak bone."

Indignation flared in her eyes. "You're wrong."

She moved toward the door as if to leave, but he blocked her escape.

"Answer me something," he said, brushing a strand of hair behind her ear. "When you decided to come back, how many new rules did you make up to keep me from getting too close to you and Will?"

Her eyes widened.

If he hadn't been paying attention, he'd have missed her reaction. But he'd seen it and knew he'd scored a point. So much for not keeping score.

James removed his Resistol, then ran his hand through his hair and blew out a frustrated breath before replacing his hat. "That's what I thought. If we're going to make this work, then we've got to call a truce."

A red blush colored her cheeks. Her chin thrust forward. She turned back to the horse. "I didn't come here looking for trouble, but I had no way of knowing if you'd welcome Will and me. I only want to protect him."

He wondered if she would ever put aside her stupid rules and trust him.

She had once. Maybe she would again. Only, time wasn't on his side. Not where Kelly was concerned.

Placing his hands on her shoulders, he turned her to face him. He needed to regain her respect. "Do you really think I'd hurt my son? Or you?"

Kelly stared at the center of his chest. "I've been gone quite a while. I didn't know what to expect."

"I really do want to help, but I can't, not if you keep pushing me away like you've been doing. Like you're doing now," James said, willing her to look at him. "What do you say? Are you agreeable to a truce?"

"Yes. I don't want to argue anymore."

"Me, neither. And one other thing, I'm more than a little concerned about you. To tell the truth, you look like hell. As soon as you get a clean bill of health from the doctor, you can start to work."

Admitting susceptibility of any kind didn't come easy to Kelly. There were too many times as a foster child when her very existence had depended on her strength, her ability to hide any vulnerability. Disclosing certain information to James was the last thing Kelly wanted to do. Rule number five: never reveal a weakness, lest it be turned against you.

She stood close enough to see the gold flecks in James's brown eyes and felt more defenseless than she had in a long time. At Sara's prompting she had left Will inside so she and James could talk. Only now, being this close to him, she needed reaffirmation of why it was necessary to stay with James.

She wanted to choose her words carefully. "I'm just tired. You're overreacting. It's really not a big deal." At his scowl, she reinforced her statement. "I promise."

His attention didn't waver. "Company policy."

She sighed, wishing he wouldn't look at her like that, as if he could see into her soul. If only she could think of a way to appease his curiosity without telling him what she feared, that there was something terribly wrong with her. Did she dare trust him? She'd barely survived the last time she'd trusted him.

Kelly tried to ignore the intensity in James's eyes. "Since Will's birth, there have been so many things to do—classes, homework, my job and taking care of Will. I've done my best to maintain a high grade-point average and studied every spare minute, which wasn't often. It seemed I was always behind. Sometimes I'd study all night, trying to catch up. I guess I overdid it while studying for finals."

James caught her chin between his thumb and forefinger, tipping her face back while he studied her. "You've got dark circles under your eyes. You're pale. And you're so thin a strong wind would blow you away. You're not working until you see a doctor," he said, moving closer, his breath warm on her cheek.

His nearness overwhelmed her. Kelly stumbled back against the horse to stop the sudden racing of her heart. "O-okay, but honestly it's nothing, really."

"You've got to take care of yourself. Who'll be there for Will if something happens to you?"

That he had the foresight to think of her son shocked Kelly. It was also why she'd come, but she didn't want to press James about Will until he'd had time to fall in love with him. "Nothing's wrong with me that a good night's sleep won't fix."

His gaze roamed the contours of her face. "You've had a good night's sleep, and you still look awful."

"Gee, thanks," she said, trying not to react to his

close scrutiny. "You always did know how to flatter a woman."

"You said you always make decisions based on Will's best interest."

"That's right." She wondered what he was getting at.

"You think pushing yourself until you drop is what's best for him?"

She looked away. "I'm all right, James. Really. Finals are over, and I have three months before school resumes."

"Yeah, sure," he said, stepping closer, ignoring that she'd backed away from him. "Let me know when your appointment is. I'm going with you."

Her eyes widened. "What?"

"If you won't take care of yourself, then I will. What kind of future will our son have if you kill yourself?" he asked, moving a few wild hairs away from her face. His touch shook her, making her stomach clench, her heart pound. "I want to help you, Kel. Let me take care of you."

Kelly's breath caught, whether from his words or his touch, she didn't know. She thought to lean away from his long fingers, but instead moved toward them. "What do you mean?"

He shrugged. "I don't know exactly, but I want to help. And not just for the next three months. I don't want you killing yourself just to get by."

She stared at him, unable to form a complete thought.

His hand caught her nape. His callused thumb brushed back and forth across her cheek, stoking the fire of his touch. "I'd have done it before now if you'd just told me about Will."

"Why?" The word came out thick, husky.

"Because I care."

His head dipped toward hers. He brushed her lips with his. Though she wanted to give in to the kiss, Kelly shoved a splayed hand in the center of his chest. "Wait! Fifteen minutes ago we were talking about Will. How did we get to this point?"

He didn't bother to look contrite, unsettling her even more. One corner of his mouth lifted in a crooked smile. "Guess it's just the force of nature."

Kelly stared at James's back as he turned and walked away. *Force of nature?* That disturbed her. Almost as much as the way her traitorous body ached for his touch, his kisses, to be in his arms, as if it was the most natural thing in the world.

As if that's where she really belonged.

After glancing at the assembly instructions for the crib, James frowned at the leftover screws and washers. He shrugged and handed the paper to Will. "Here, partner, why don't you look at this and tell me if you can make heads or tails of what it says." James slid beneath the bed he'd bought for Will on the way home from Cal's and tightened the screws that held the mattress frame in place.

Will hunkered down at the side of the baby bed and looked at James sprawled on his back.

"Did you already figure it all out?" James pulled the hammer out of reach of the boy's small hand and dropped it in his toolbox beside him.

Will crawled beneath the bed and tried to get on James's chest, bumping his head in the process. Then the kid flopped over onto the floor, his head making a loud thunk as it hit the wood.

James winced and peeked from the corner of his eye to see if the boy was hurt. He smiled when Will began to point and jabber. "Gook dat."

Kelly had already translated that particular term that seemed to be Will's favorite choice of words these days, so James knew Will was telling him to look at something or other.

"Uh-huh." He slid another screw into position and turned it.

Will rolled over, his boot catching James in the gut. When he could draw oxygen into his lungs, he glanced over at the child, who was happy as a new colt. "A fella can get hurt turning his back on you."

Will nodded and pointed at the screwdriver James held. "Gook dat."

"Yep. We're about done here and need to go feed the horses."

"Horsey," Will said, his head bobbing up and down as if on a spring.

"You really like going outside and feeding the horses, don't you?"

"Ow-side." Will backed from under the bed, bumping his head again on the side of the crib in the process.

James winced as he slid out and watched his son rub the area he'd whacked. "Does it hurt? You got it pretty good that time." He touched the spot where Will's hand had been, the boy's hair sleek as a show horse's coat beneath James's fingers. His chest tightened, and a knot settled in his throat. He was glad Kelly had agreed to stay here with him. It would give Will a chance to have memories of doing things with him, something James didn't have with his own dad.

He ducked as Will plopped in his lap. Though he

tried to get out of the way, Will bonked his head on James's chin. "Ouch."

James rubbed his jaw, waiting to see if Will had been hurt by their collision. He looked down at his son, dressed in miniature blue jeans, Western shirt and four-inch long boots. Will. His son. The warmth in his chest spread like a pasture fire in August.

Unlike his own father, who had dressed him in fatigues at this age and tried to turn him into a soldier who followed orders, James wanted Will to be a child. To his way of thinking, little boys shouldn't have to adhere to a strict code of behavior where they had to do everything at a certain time as if life was a precision drill.

As a child James had never been allowed to tag along when his father went to the base. Even when his homework and chores were done, James wasn't allowed to do as he pleased with his spare time. More than anything else *that* was the one thing he wanted most. For Will to run free.

"Is Will in here with you?" Kelly came into the room, her steps clipped, a worried frown on her face as she wiped the remnants of sleep from her eyes.

James twisted so she could see the boy seated on his lap. "Will's been helping me put the bed together while you took a nap. I just need to drop the mattress in, and it's all set."

Kelly hurried over and took the child. "I'm sorry, James. I'll try to keep him from bothering you. I didn't mean to fall asleep. But even if I'm awake, he slips away so fast, it's hard to keep track of where he's gone."

Pushing himself to his feet, James said. "Don't apologize. You needed to rest. Besides, Will's no problem. I've spent some time around Cal's daughter, and though Jessie is a little younger, she still can be a handful.''

In that moment James realized what he said was true. Being around Will hadn't been a problem. In fact, he got a kick out of watching the child and the way he found everything so fascinating.

''Well, okay, but let me know if he gets in your way.''

''He won't,'' he said, glancing at his watch. ''We're headed out now to feed the horses.''

Will's eyes widened and lit up with excitement. ''Horsey.'' He squirmed in an effort to get down and finally leaned toward James, his arms outstretched.

James caught Will beneath his arms and lifted him. ''I'll set up the bed we bought for you when we come back inside.'' He grinned. ''Unless you've changed your mind.''

Kelly shook her head, but James saw the threatening smile. ''Friends don't sleep together.''

He shrugged, finally admitting to himself how much he wanted to be more than just her friend. The next three months were going to be tough. It would be easier if he and Kelly didn't agree on most things or if they fought all the time. But they didn't. Or at least they never had until he had discovered what she'd done. Now they were both tense, unsure and wary. And he hated that.

The things she'd made him feel scared him. And that hadn't changed, even now that he knew about Will. He could hardly blame her for doubting him. After all, he had never been the settling kind. She'd had no way of knowing how much she'd affected him that night. And now she'd come back, wanting nothing more than to be his friend.

She'd slipped away from him once, but wouldn't be so lucky this time. This time James intended to regain her respect. No matter what it took. And from the look of things, that was going to be a hell of a lot harder than taking care of Will.

If he could accomplish that, then maybe he could figure out a way to make Kelly want to be more than just his friend.

He had once. Maybe he could again.

Chapter Five

The next morning James glanced up from a chart as the bell over the door chimed. Kelly entered the clinic office looking as though she'd lost her last friend.

Circling the counter, he dropped the chart and caught her by the shoulders. The urge to hold her close knotted his gut. "What's wrong? Where's Will?"

"Preschool," she said, her chin quivering. "Since I was able to get an appointment with the doctor at eleven, I went ahead and enrolled him this morning."

"If you're this upset, I'm going with you to your appointment."

"That's not it." She sniffed. "I know it's really stupid for me to be upset, but he didn't cry."

James frowned. He didn't understand at all what she was talking about. "You mean Will? He didn't cry about what?"

"Will always fusses when I leave him. Today I took him into the room for the children his age. When he saw the other kids, he got so excited, he almost jumped out of my arms. In fact, when I tried to kiss him goodbye, he pushed me away and ran to play with his new friends.'' Her feeble attempt at a smile wobbled and collapsed, then she walked into James's arms.

Comprehension dawned, and James held her tight. His chin settled on her head. The need to comfort her consumed him. ''Hon, the boy just wants to play with kids his own age. You ought to be thrilled.''

''I am, I think. It's just that I've been everything to him. He always pitches a fit when I leave him. Today he couldn't wait to get away from me. I don't think he even noticed when I left.''

James lifted her chin with his forefinger. ''You think that means Will doesn't love you anymore?''

She chewed her bottom lip. ''I don't think it's that he doesn't love me, but he doesn't need me so much.''

He had never seen this side of Kelly before, the insecurity, uncertainty. ''Trust me. By the end of the day he'll be chompin' at the bit for you to take him home.'' He cupped her face. ''You feeling okay now?''

Kelly stared up at him. He was suddenly as lost as a new foal. Leaning toward her, he promised himself he wouldn't kiss her again. But that's exactly what he did.

James then decided it would be a kiss between friends, a no-big-deal kiss—one that didn't count. Only that didn't happen, either.

Kelly's lips were full and wet beneath his. Sweet and responsive. He deepened the kiss, needing to feel her softness, her response. He groaned, slipping his tongue between her parted lips. When she moaned into his mouth, making those little noises in the back of her throat, whatever good intentions he'd had went out the window.

His hands settled on her hips. He pulled her closer, aching for her touch. The feel of her against him. His tongue thrust in and out until she leaned toward him. Her scent, her taste, drove him to the brink of insanity. He backed her against the wall, clinging to her... waiting, needing...

The eight-second buzzer sounded.

Realizing it was the bell over the door, James released Kelly and took a step back, then caught her when her knees buckled.

Sara paused in the doorway. "Oh. Am I interrupting something?"

Kelly blinked several times. "Hmm? What?"

"Is this a bad time?" Sara asked.

Kelly gave James a chastising look and ran the back of her hand across her lips, still wet and swollen from his kiss. "Uh, no, not at all. Actually, you're timing is perfect."

James could think of a lot of things to call Sara's timing. *Perfect* wasn't among them.

He cursed his lack of control around Kelly. It irritated him that he couldn't seem to think straight when she was near or keep his hands off her. She would never believe he had changed if he didn't learn restraint.

"The preschool is everything you said it would be," Kelly told Sara. "I really thought Will would fuss about staying, but he hardly noticed me leaving."

"I take Jessie one day a week so she'll be around other children. That gives me a chance to get the clinic's books caught up," Sara said.

"So, which preschool is he at?" James asked.

"Miss Clancy's Little People." Kelly reached for a coffee mug with hands that shook. She dropped it, and the cup clanked against the table. "The one we decided on last night," she said, picking up the mug.

"If you've got a minute, Kelly," Sara said, "I'd like to show you how I do the books."

Kelly poured a cup of coffee and retrieved a package of artificial sweetener which she tossed unopened into the trash. She stirred the contents of the mug and followed Sara into the next room.

James was pleased to note that Kelly, too, had been affected by the kiss. Served her right.

In the brief time since her return, she'd invaded every aspect of his life. Her lipstick lined his favorite coffee mugs. Her perfumed soap had run him out of his own shower. And when he'd searched his clothes dryer for a clean pair of jeans, he'd pulled out a silk thong that had kicked his libido into turbo overdrive.

Being her friend, keeping his distance, was going to make it a helluva long three months.

James stood and tossed the third magazine he'd thumbed through onto the waiting room table. He didn't understand why Kelly had thrown such a fit over him going back with her to see the doctor. It wasn't as if he'd never seen her without her clothes. When she'd argued that it had only been the one night, he'd countered by asking her if she had something she was hiding. He still thought she'd overreacted.

In the end Kelly had won. A nurse that reminded him of a cantankerous bull had chased him from the examination room to wait out front.

After checking his watch for the fifth time since

he'd begun his vigil, James began to pace. What could be taking so long?

Just as he was about to ask about Kelly at the front desk, the door at the other end of the office opened and Kelly rushed out. She passed him quickly, thrusting the bill at him and kept on going, but not before he saw the tears pooled in her eyes.

"Kel, wait."

She marched through the glass door and out of the office.

James withdrew his wallet and pulled out a couple of bills as he approached the receptionist. He wanted to follow Kelly, and barely controlled himself while waiting for the clerk to write a receipt.

He hurried outside and into the parking lot, but didn't see her. Then he heard a whimper and circled his truck.

He found Kelly doubled over behind the cab on the passenger's side. Her arms circled her middle while her wrenching sobs called up his need to comfort and protect her.

The urge to take her in his arms and hold her finally propelled him forward. He needed to do something—anything—to stop her tears and ease her pain before it consumed him.

Something was dreadfully wrong, but he didn't know what. He'd seen Kelly tear up a time or two over the years, but nothing like this. Whatever had caused this wasn't good, and since she'd just come from the doctor's office, he wasn't sure he wanted to know what it was.

When he touched her, Kelly walked into his arms and buried her head against his chest. Her tears wet his shirt, but he didn't care. All that mattered right now was her. So for the next five minutes he held her until her tears had almost subsided.

He lifted her chin and eased the pads of his thumbs across her cheeks to dry her tears. Crying had turned her nose red and clumped her lashes together. "You ready to go?" he asked.

"Yes."

James opened the door and helped her inside, then hurried around the pickup and slid behind the wheel. Without saying a word, he started his truck, put it in gear and drove out of the parking lot. Then he hooked his arm around her shoulders and pulled her to his side.

Neither said a word on the drive to the pond behind his house. They used to come here a lot, but that had been before she'd left. Shutting the truck off, he got out and helped her to the ground. Together they started toward the edge of the water, and their fingers somehow ended up woven together.

"You want to tell me what that was all about?"

"I'm happy."

James stopped, his hold on her hand pulling her back. "What?"

"I'm not going to die."

"You thought you were dying?"

She let go of his hand and approached the water's edge.

He came up behind her and rested his palms on her shoulders. "Kel, I know you've been feeling bad, but did you really think it was that serious?"

She nodded.

James turned her to face him. "Tell me about it."

"You won't like it," she said, glancing up at him.

"Never stopped you from speaking your mind before."

"I guess you're right."

James pulled her to the back of his truck and once he'd lowered the tailgate, they both took a seat. "Okay, shoot."

"A long time ago I made friends with this older couple, Mr. and Mrs. Mathews. They were the kindest people, but they were getting up there in age. Mr. Mathews started feeling bad. He was always tired and sometimes had some problems with disorientation and some dizziness. I started having those same symptoms while I was studying for finals."

James caught Kelly's hand in his. "What did he have?"

"I don't know. I was barely a teenager, and even if I did hear, I don't remember what it was."

He opened Kelly's hand, palm up and ran his thumb across the hollow. "What happened to him?"

It was a moment before she said anything, making James wonder if she'd heard him.

"He died."

The hurt in her voice told James that Mr. Mathews had been more than just a friend. He didn't know how he knew, but he sensed her painful loss.

The thought of something similar happening to Kelly made his shoulders tighten. He stood and pulled Kelly to her feet, settling his hands at her waist so she couldn't try to get away without telling him what he wanted to hear. "What did the doctor say about you? And I want specifics."

A blush rose to her cheeks. "I feel really stupid telling you this. I guess I got scared and just didn't think."

"What?"

"He said I was anemic. He ran a blood test to confirm that. That's why it took so long."

James got weak in the knees and light-headed all at the same time. He wanted to shout with relief. "I'm glad that's all it was. Did he give you a prescription for iron?"

"Yeah, I put it in my pocket. Oh, and I need to reimburse you for my doctor bill. I'm sorry I overreacted. I was just so relieved. I was so sure I would end up the same way as Mr. Mathews."

He paused a minute. "Kelly, you said I wouldn't like what you were going to tell me. Is that all it was? That you thought you were going to die?"

Kelly swallowed hard. "I came back here because I thought something terrible was wrong with me. And I wanted your promise that you'd raise Will."

James felt as if she'd kicked him the gut. "Did you think so little of me that you believed I wouldn't care for him?"

The challenge in her eyes surprised him. "There are thousands of children in foster care whose parents don't want them."

"Not my child." He dropped his hands from her waist and turned back toward the water. "The day will never come when I wouldn't want Will."

He sensed Kelly behind him before she placed her hand on his back. "I was afraid to believe that you would do the right thing. I misjudged you, and I'm sorry."

He expected to feel satisfied, but he didn't. "So, what now, Kelly?"

"What do you mean?"

He turned to face her. "Will you be leaving now that you know you're not dying?"

"No, James. I know I was wrong not to tell you about Will. I want Will to know his father. We'll stay through the summer as originally planned."

James nodded, unable to speak for the emotion that had filled his throat at the thought of losing the son he had just discovered. And losing her again.

If that prospect was this difficult now, what would he do when they left at the end of the summer?

Kelly glanced at Will, who had jabbered ninety-to-nothing since she'd picked him up from preschool that evening. "I take it you had a good time today and made lots of new friends to play with?" she asked, settling the peanut butter sandwich in front of him.

Will nodded, avoiding her hand as she tried to brush his hair off his forehead. He grabbed half the sandwich and clutched it in his fist. "Play."

She hadn't realized how much Will looked like James until she'd seen them side by side. There were the obvious resemblances like eye and hair color. But even now she could see Will would sport the same long, lanky frame as his dad, the same dark handsomeness that made women take second glances and the same mouth, perfect for kissing. She frowned and turned back to the counter to make another sandwich.

The front door opened and closed, and she looked over her shoulder as James strolled into the kitchen. He squatted down beside Will, who launched into a new indistinguishable litany of his daily activities. She tried not to notice the way James's dark hair brushed his nape beneath his Resistol or how his denim shirt strained across his shoulders.

Will pushed his sandwich under James's nose, offering him a bite.

She watched, waiting to see what James would do and was surprised when he took a bite and said, "Mmm. Peanut butter and jelly. Again."

Then Will dropped the sandwich he'd had a stranglehold on and held his arms out to James. "Horsey."

James swiveled on his heel to glance at Kelly. "Is he through eating?"

His question had been innocent enough, but the way his intense gaze seemed to caress every part of her made it difficult to think. He'd always had that effect on her. She didn't know who she was more disgusted with, him for looking or herself for bothering to notice—or worse, her body for responding.

Kelly tried to ignore the feelings of longing, but failed. "Will can't sit still long enough to eat an entire meal. He usually runs around a while, then comes back for a nibble or two before dashing off again. I guess it's more like grazing."

James lifted Will in his arms and strolled across the kitchen toward her. He paused an arm's length away, his gaze lingering on her cheek. "Did the doctor say anything about you working?"

"Yeah. He said I could work regular hours. The iron pills and a healthy diet should fix me right up. So, can I come back to work tomorrow?" He was getting to her, looking at her like that. She snatched up a wet washcloth and wiped Will's hands, anything to keep from noticing how good James looked, how wonderful he smelled. Or admitting she wanted to be pulled into his strong arms.

"Why don't you rest tomorrow and come in the day after." James looked at her and smiled. He bent forward, as she wiped her son's palm, to kiss the spot he'd stared at moments before.

Her heart slammed against her ribs. Her legs threatened to collapse, and she grabbed at the counter to keep from falling.

He straightened, then brushed his thumb across where his lips had been. "Mmm. Never tasted so good before."

"What are you doing?" Her words came out thick and rough.

A smile tipped up the corners of his mouth. "You had peanut butter on your cheek. I think I got it all."

She pushed his hand away and scrubbed the dish towel across her cheek to rid herself of his lingering touch, only it didn't work. "Would you like me to make you a sandwich?"

He brushed a strand of hair behind her ear. "No, I had a late lunch on the way back to the office after stopping at the McCarthy place."

Kelly wished he'd move back another step or two or ten. She turned to retrieve the tablet beside the sink. "I've started a list of things."

"Why does that not surprise me?" James looked at Will who seemed totally content to be held by his dad. "Whatever it is, forget it. The house is fine. You're going to rest while you're here."

Kelly knew she shouldn't look at him, but she did and regretted it immediately when he turned his more-sinful-than-chocolate gaze on her.

"Not a list of things to clean," she hurried to explain, "this is stuff I need to pick up, like diapers and more training pants for Will. I'm trying to ease him into potty training—"

"Do what?"

"Toilet training. I'm trying to get him used to sitting on the pot, so whenever I change him, I put him on his potty chair. If he ever uses it for you, be sure to praise him."

"Do you need anything else?" he asked, closing the fingers of his free hand over hers, totally ignoring the detailed list she had so carefully made.

"No." The word came out sounding strained.

"I'll stop at the store on my way home tomorrow. I'm going to fix dinner." He stuck the list in his pocket, then cocked his head to the side as Will pulled James's Resistol off and settled it on his own head. "I want you to make yourself at home."

"I will. Thank you." *Home.* Somehow the word sounded false, because, as much as she'd like, this would never be her home. It was only temporary, just like everything else in her life.

She turned her back on James and wiped the counter. "Have you ever wanted something so much you were willing to sacrifice anything to get it?"

"Yeah," he said. "But sometimes, even after making the sacrifice, you walk away empty-handed."

She heard the soul-wrenching sadness in his voice.

"I suppose." Kelly couldn't help but wonder what he had wanted that he didn't get. It always seemed to her that while she'd struggled for every little thing, James had always gotten everything he wanted with little or no effort.

"What is it that you want so bad?" he asked.

Kelly turned back to face him. "Well, one day when I can afford it, I'd like a new truck."

"If you want one that bad," he said, "I can always get it for you."

"No. I was thinking somewhere down the road. I figure mine's got another five or six years left in it."

James gave her a skeptical look. "Speaking of your truck, I don't like the idea of you driving anywhere late at night in it." He fished his keys from his pocket, reining Kelly's thoughts in, drawing her attention to that cursed buckle, a reminder of everything that had happened that night. The night they had made Will.

He'd been so proud of *that* buckle. It had attracted the opposite sex like bees to honey. If Kelly had been able, she'd have left the rodeo rather than stay to witness James's adoration by the tight-jeaned throng, but she'd ridden there with him and so she'd waited.

Maybe it had been the heady combination of all that pent-up emotion and the excitement of his win, but on the way home their hands had brushed and sparks had flown.

"Kelly?"

She realized then that James had said something about her truck.

"I'm sorry?" Kelly couldn't believe she sounded so calm. The direction of her thoughts, his nearness, made her insides feel as taut as a lead rope with a skittish mare on the other end.

"If you need to go anywhere at night, you can take my truck."

"Your truck?" Being inside his pickup to relive the events of that night was the last thing she wanted.

"Or I could drive you."

"No." She hadn't meant to shout, but being in his truck with him alone at night would make her think of things she would just as soon forget. Things like how he'd pulled her across the seat to sit close to his side. And as they'd barreled up Interstate 35, he'd slipped his arm around her, tipped her chin up and kissed her. It hadn't been much of a kiss really, just a hurried brush of his lips over hers. But it was something she'd wanted for such a long time, and the liquid heat of his mouth had made her come all undone.

Then he'd pulled over to the side of the road and kissed her so thoroughly she hadn't realized until afterward where his hands had gone. Or hers.

No, being in his truck was certainly the last thing she needed tonight. "I'm not planning on going anywhere."

"If you do, I'd like you to take me. Otherwise, I'd be worried until you got home." He lifted his hat from where it wobbled on Will's head and settled it low on his own brow before going out the back door, her son on his hip.

Kelly closed her eyes. She longed to run after him, but didn't. What could she say that hadn't already been said? It was too late to change what had happened between them.

Once before she had given in to her desire to be loved by him, and it had cost her their friendship. She wouldn't make that same mistake again. No matter how much she might want it.

Even after mucking out all the stalls and spreading fresh hay, James's frustration remained.

He had never worried much about relationships. Getting a date had never been a big deal. The ratio of buckle bunnies to rodeoers was probably twenty-to-one. Finding someone willing to change her plans for the night had never been hard. Until now.

And that was part of the problem. He had no idea where to begin with Kelly, what to do or say to regain her respect, make her forget what had happened and once again see him as she had before she'd left.

James had always done what he wanted, when he wanted, where he wanted. He refused to stand by while some woman charged in, making lists and spouting rules. His father had certainly made both their lives miserable, trying to make James into a career soldier, but he hadn't succeeded. And if the sergeant major had failed to force James to conform, what chance did a slip of a woman like Kelly have?

Besides, James was happy with things as they were. He and Cal had the clinic. He and the bank owned the ranch, complete with cattle. He had everything a man could want.

Except he had a woman who wanted to be only friends.

Okay, so he wanted Kelly. It wasn't as if he needed her. Not the way he needed to rodeo every now and then to prove he still had what it took.

The reason he'd gone after Kelly when she'd left was because they'd been good friends. He'd shared things with her he'd never revealed to anyone else. Now that she'd returned, he had to finally admit what he hadn't wanted to acknowledge before. He had done his best to forget her after she'd gone. And he'd failed.

He didn't want to be *just* friends anymore, but if that's all Kelly wanted, then he would have to figure out a way to make it work.

James had been high on his championship win their only time together, and that must have been the reason everything had gotten out of perspective. He couldn't help but wonder if making love to her once more would make the gnawing in his gut go away. Maybe then he could get his life back to its normal disorder the way he liked it. Except now he wanted his life to include Will.

He glanced over his shoulder at his son. Watching Will made James feel things he'd never experienced, see things as if for the first time and want things he'd never wanted before now.

The child tossed hay in the air, then turned in circles as it fell around him. He shadowed James's every step, mimicked his every movement and chattered like a magpie. At first the boy's constant noise had driven James nuts, making him want to run and hide. But at some point, and he wasn't exactly sure when it had happened, he'd begun to understand some of what the kid said. Now they actually carried on one-word conversations with each other.

And when Will played, James felt as if he watched a newborn foal discovering in innocent wonder everything different and new in the world. Watching Will get dirty and do all the things James had never been allowed to do as a child made him feel good. He wondered if Kelly would be mad when she saw Will's grass-stained clothes, but that's why they'd invented bleach. James didn't plan to let anyone rein in his boy, not the way his dad had him.

He knelt on one knee beside his son. "You about ready to go inside?"

Will paused in his twirling to shake his head, grabbing at James when he had trouble finding his balance after all the spinning.

James splayed his hand across the boy's back and marveled at the differences in their size. Hard to believe Will might be his size one day.

The lad gave him a look he could only describe as mischievous before bolting from the stall. Will raced from the barn, glancing over his shoulder to see if James followed.

He smiled and hurried after Will, catching him easily. Then he carried him like a football under his arm into the house. Kelly might have a fit if she saw Will running loose. Most times she wouldn't let him step one foot outside the house without holding his hand or attaching a blasted kiddie leash to him. But James refused to harness the boy.

Come to think of it, Kelly had never said anything about him taking Will outside. And, thankfully, she hadn't insisted he use the harness. He didn't think that was something he could ever do.

James lowered Will to his feet. "Kelly?"

When he got no response, he checked the living room and then the bedroom where he found her curled on her side, sound asleep, with the blue notebook he'd seen in her truck and a pen beside her.

He hated the thought of waking her up and decided to let her sleep. Slipping the notebook from beneath her hand, he moved it and the pen to the nightstand. He stared at it for a moment and considered looking inside, then decided it was probably nothing more than her lists. And besides, it really wasn't any of his business.

She would probably want him to wake her up for instructions about getting Will ready for bed, but he wasn't going to. He turned the light off and slipped from the room.

Maybe if he looked around, he'd find a detailed list. She had always been real big on making lists. If he could change one thing about her, it would be her penchant for creating rules by which to live.

James noticed it was nine o'clock and figured it was

getting close to Will's bedtime. He knew Sara usually put Jessie down pretty early. Then he remembered Kelly saying something about putting the boy on the pot.

Will ran in circles like a barrel racer. He didn't look at all tired to James.

James squatted down and caught Will around the waist. "You ready to drain the lizard?"

Ten minutes later Will still refused to go to the bathroom. When James squatted beside the boy to explain what he wanted, his son just shook his head. Now what?

Finally after another ten minutes of waiting without success, Will stood, his jeans pooled around his ankles. He shuffled to James and paused as if undecided. Then, he slipped his arms around James's neck and hugged him.

James's chest grew tight. A lump the size of a saddle settled in his throat. And without thought or question, he slid his arms around his son and hugged him back. It felt good, and James knew he'd do anything to protect the boy from harm...and Kelly's rules.

At least now Will would have James on his side when Kelly tried to stifle the boy, something he wished he'd had growing up. But his mom had been too afraid of his father to argue. She'd begged James to keep the peace by following his father's dictates, something he never did get the hang of. Even now that still stuck in his craw.

Never would James make any overly restrictive demands of his son. He intended to see that Will had the opportunity to grow up knowing his own mind, being his own person, following his own dream.

Kelly's rules be hanged.

Chapter Six

"Spencer Jefferson's high-dollar mare is in labor and having trouble. You want to tag along?" James asked, walking in the back door.

Kelly's head snapped up, her eyes wide. "Oh." The pen she'd been writing with fell from her fingers, and she placed her hand over the page.

"Didn't mean to scare you."

"I thought you'd already left."

He walked toward her. "What's in the notebook?"

She closed it, then placed one hand over it as if to keep him from opening it. "Oh, nothing, really."

Nothing? James didn't think so. She was acting too skittish, as if she'd been caught with her hand in the cookie jar. "Is that your book of rules?"

Kelly pushed back her chair and stood. "You said Spencer Jefferson's mare is having trouble?"

"Yeah," he said, dismissing the notebook. "You want to go with me?"

"Is this the mare he got right before I left that had the entire county in an uproar?"

"Yeah. He bred her to Sam Dunlap's champion stallion."

"Oh, yeah, I'm going. Will's in day care all day. You couldn't keep me away." She stood and grabbed the notebook, then hurried down the hall to his spare bedroom where he'd set up the new bed they'd bought her. In no time she marched past him and headed out the door. "I want to see this foal. I bet it's a beaut."

James followed her outside, trying to ignore how nice her backside looked in the jeans she wore today. Made a man want to— *Whoa.* He'd better learn to get a grip on the way she made him feel.

Kelly paused and gave him an uneasy look. "Let's take my truck."

"Nah. I've already got mine loaded. Come on."

She looked as though she wanted to argue, but finally shrugged and climbed into his pickup.

On the drive to Spencer's, James tried to concentrate on the thick brush lining the road and the green leaves cloaking the oak trees. Instead his mind turned to Kelly. *What had all that been about? The hesitancy and the notebook? What was she hiding from him now?*

Five minutes later he parked beside Spencer's barn and climbed out. Even with his long legs, he found himself eating Kelly's dust as she hurried inside.

Once in the barn, James shook Spencer's hand and headed into the large stall. He'd stayed in some hotel rooms that weren't this big or plush.

After checking the mare, he glanced at Spencer. "How long's she been like this?"

"I think about four hours," Spencer said, rubbing

the horse's neck. "She was like this when I came out this morning."

James pulled a syringe from his bag. "I'm going to give her an injection of oxytocin to make her contractions stronger."

"Can that hurt the foal?" Spencer asked, his concern obvious.

"I'd say the odds of that happening are not nearly as high as her going on this way the rest of the day, trying to push that baby out."

"All right. Listen, I've got some other chores I can't put off. I'll leave my cell phone on," Spencer said as he moved to the door and paused. "Give me a call if she foals or you need me to come back."

"It will probably be a while, but I'll give you a call."

After Spencer had left, Kelly moved to stroke the mare's head. "That's all right, honey, I can sympathize with what you're going through, even if these guys can't."

"How long were you in labor with Will?"

"Twelve long, grueling hours."

She had a wistful look on her face and James knew she was remembering Will's delivery, a memory he'd never be able to share. "Did you have a hard time?"

"Well, I didn't ask for drugs if that's what you mean," Kelly said with a grin, "but there was a time or two when I wanted to hit someone."

James smiled. He had no trouble envisioning Kelly, her hair wet from her exertion, her temper frayed, her belly swollen with his child.

"As long as I'm confessing, I did scream once," she admitted. "Maybe twice. Actually, it was probably closer to five times." She smiled. "In fact, I'm surprised you didn't hear me bellowing all the way down here.''

"I hate that you went through it alone. If I'd known, I would have come."

Her gaze held no blame or recrimination. "I know you would've, but I got through it okay."

"Kelly, I know you're strong, but that's one time you shouldn't have been alone."

"That's something I can't take back now."

It was after lunch when the foal's nose and front feet came into view. "Here we go," James said. He assisted when the foal slid free with the next contraction.

All business now, James and Kelly worked together to make sure the baby was breathing okay.

As the mare cleaned her baby and the colt tried to gain its wobbly legs, James caught Kelly's shoulders and pulled her back against him. Together they stood watching as the baby tried its first tentative step.

"I wish I'd been there for Will's first steps," James said. "There's so much I've missed, so many things Will's done without my being there to see them. I don't want anything else to happen without me being there for my son." And for Kelly, too.

Kelly turned to look at him. "James, I'm sorry."

"I'm not saying these things to hurt you, Kel. I'm just telling you how I feel."

After a long, lingering look that tore at his heart, she turned back to watch the colt.

It was the same expression she'd worn this morning when he'd caught her writing in the notebook. Somehow he didn't think it contained a list of her rules.

Funny that they should be here together again. In spite of her rules, he had to admit he'd missed her something awful. Sometimes it had felt as though she'd taken a big chunk of him with her when she'd left. He couldn't help but wonder if she had ever thought about him at all. Maybe just once.

"You did a good job here today," she said.

"So did you, but then you've always been a hard worker. Thanks for your help."

"We make a good team."

They always had.

Apparently, they still did.

Kelly stood at the end of the couch and stared.

The father of her child, the one-time object of her affection, lay sprawled across the divan.

He wore nothing but an old pair of jeans, worn soft with age, frayed around the bottoms from his boot heels and spurs. His bare feet hung over one armrest. And cradled in his arms was the child they'd made together.

She couldn't have moved if she'd wanted to. This was only one of many reasons why she'd put off coming back. Heart pounding, she looked her fill. And now, with no one to witness her longing, she admitted that everything she'd told herself about James since leaving had been a lie. She still wanted him. Always had wanted him. Probably *would* always want him.

And on top of all that, earlier today after the colt had been born, James had talked about missing Will's first steps and other firsts. It had broken her heart to see such a strong man hurting. She'd finally had to turn away, because if she'd looked at him any longer, she might have spilled her guts.

Kelly told herself sharing the colt's delivery had made them both emotional. She tried to ignore the need to feel James's touch. It had been a long day and an even longer night. Sitting close to James while watching TV had gotten to her, and she'd slipped out to the front porch.

Now Kelly stood staring at the dark hair falling over James's brow. It had a tendency to sweep forward onto his forehead, like Will's. She reached out to brush it back, but paused. The idea of touching him even in sleep sent a wave of heat through her, followed immediately by an intense rush of longing that made her gasp.

James stirred and blinked up at her. "What time is it?" Sleep made his voice husky, sexy.

Kelly braced herself against the stampede of memories and glanced at her watch. "Midnight."

"What are you doing up?"

She shrugged. "I'm restless."

His brows furrowed. "You feeling okay?"

"Yeah. I'm fine." Kelly lifted Will. She needed to touch her son before putting him to bed. Also to put distance between her and James.

James's hand brushed her breast as he tried to pull it from around Will.

She gasped. Her flesh tightened.

Giving her a knowing smile, James freed his hand. He sat up. "Before I fell asleep I was thinking about you driving Will around in your old truck. Do you have a cell phone in case you break down?"

"I don't need a cell phone. And my truck isn't going to break down."

She held Will close and inhaled his familiar little-boy scent. It helped ease the tension eating at her. "What's the deal with you suddenly worrying about my truck breaking down? I've had no trouble with it."

James ran a hand over his chin, his whisker stubble making a rasping sound. "I'm just watching out for you. Why don't you carry my phone for now? I'll get you one."

"That's ridiculous. I can't afford one." She started toward the hall, intending to get some distance between her and James by putting Will to bed.

"The clinic will get it."

She paused and turned back. "Don't be silly. I don't want or need a cell phone."

One brow shot up. "Why? Because I suggested it?"

"Of course not." Kelly tried to calm herself and leaned her cheek against Will's head. "Look, James, I don't need you to take care of me. I've done just fine on my own."

"Humor me."

"No way." She gave him a weary smile before hurrying down the hall to her room. After closing the door behind her, she slumped against the wall.

Kelly knew he had noticed her response to his touch. She still tingled from the contact and cursed her traitorous body.

She admitted she'd found James attractive years ago. She still did, though she would never tell him. Everything she'd done where he was concerned had been wrong. She'd gone to his bed and forfeited their friendship, a price she wouldn't pay again.

She wanted him. All of him, including his love. And if she couldn't have that, then she'd just have to settle for being his friend and the mother of his child.

The following morning Kelly lifted Will from the kitchen floor. She didn't have to look to know James was behind her. Every part of her felt his presence.

James stood in the doorway, leaning against the jamb, staring…at her. She tried to ignore the adrenaline rush. "What?"

"Just noticing how great you look. Can't tell you've had a child."

His words made her heart race, and her arms tightened around Will, drawing strength from his presence. "Are you hungry?"

James sauntered toward the coffeepot. "You know me better than that. I've got to get my eyes open before I can eat. Remember all those early-morning emergencies we handled together before you left?"

Kelly suppressed a groan and had a strong urge to place her hands over her ears. After a sleepless night spent thinking about James, dredging up memories of their mornings together was the last thing she wanted.

He continued anyway. "You'd take the calls, then come by here to drag me out of a bed I'd just fallen into. Sometimes I hadn't even crawled between the sheets yet."

Kelly remembered everything in vivid detail, but that's something James didn't need to know. She smoothed her hand over Will's back, regaining control over her contradictory emotions. "I bought some coffee, and eggs, too. Do you want some?"

He paused, much too close for comfort, his rugged scent making her mind whirl. "You remember our mornings together, don't you?" he said in a low voice.

Not trusting her own voice, Kelly shook her head. She knew exactly what he was doing. Taunting her. Tempting her to remember.

"I'm crushed. What about the way I always begged you to ignore the call and come get in bed with me? Surely you remember that." He trailed his finger down the slope of her cheek. ''I was really only teasing you back then, but if I'd known how good we could be together, we'd have been late to every one of those early-morning calls.''

She locked her knees to keep from falling and grabbed for the edge of the table with her free hand. Why had she thought two years would make things different? His nearness still affected her as much as, if not more than, it had then.

''Did I ever tell you how good you always looked early in the morning, how much I enjoyed waking up to you?'' he said in a low, husky voice.

Her heart gave a foolish little leap. Not at all pleased with the way she reacted to James, she put Will in the high chair, then sprinkled some of the dry cereal she'd brought with her on the tray. ''No, James, you never told me. Actually, I'm surprised you recall seeing me at all, since you'd usually been out late and had trouble focusing on anything first thing in the morning.''

''So you do remember.'' Hurt shone in his eyes. ''You know I spent most of those nights tending somebody's sick horse.''

''Not every night.''

He shrugged. ''I'm not saying I never partied, Kelly, but even on those rare occasions when I tied one on, I remember every detail about you coming by the next morning. Your hair would still be damp from your shower.'' James tugged at her hair. ''You'd brush and braid it while sitting on the edge of my bed, poking me in the ribs in an effort to get me up. And you always smelled so good, like wildflowers.''

Kelly pulled the end of her braid from his grasp and tossed it over her shoulder, dismissing the pretty words that always had come so easily to him. "Are you sure you don't want something to eat?"

"I remembered you, Kelly," he said, once more fingering the curve of her jaw. "Sometimes more than I wanted. Even before we made love." His gaze moved across her bottom lip, followed by his fingertip.

Kelly's pulse doubled its rhythm.

She took a step back until she hit the table, but it did little to soothe her flustered state of mind. The butterflies that had set up flight in her stomach now felt more like caged vultures. "I, uh…"

He caught her nape and moved closer. His look consumed her, lingering on her mouth. "You shouldn't have left, Kel. We were great together."

She refused to look at him. "We were only together that one time. And I barely remember." What a liar she had become.

James's fingers tightened at the back of her neck, urging her to look at him. "That so? Maybe I should refresh your memory."

"I…I need to get Will some breakfast." Kelly didn't think she could stand much more. Her knees had turned to oatmeal, and she leaned back against the edge of the table. She willed herself to forget what had happened that night, but she couldn't. She probably never would.

James lowered his hand to his side and exhaled a long breath. "Do you ever wonder what would have happened between us if you hadn't gone?"

"No," she said, cursing the breathless quality of her voice. "We were just friends who stepped over the line."

"Were we?"

"Yes." Kelly swallowed the lump in her throat and

schooled her features, then forced herself to look at James.

Shifting his weight to the other leg, he gave her one of his sexy, come-to-my-bed grins that had always caused her normally good judgment to desert her.

"Prove it," he said with a lift of one brow.

"Forget it." She glanced at Will who sat munching the dry cereal.

James smiled again, his eyes moving over her in a way that made her light-headed. "You really do look great, Kel. Better than I remember."

Kelly sucked in air and, needing a distraction, focused on a picture of a horse on the wall behind James. "Is there something else you want?"

"Yeah."

"What is that?"

He studied her a while longer. "You."

Heat rushed to her face, but she managed a frown. "James—"

He smiled and held up both hands, palms forward. "I know. I know. Just friends."

James moved to get a cup of coffee. He settled at the table and poured Will some more cereal. "You know, Kel, seeing as how you kept Will a secret all this time, I figure you owe me one."

After placing the skillet on the burner, Kelly flipped on the heat and moved to the refrigerator. She pulled down the bowl of eggs Sara had sent with her, afraid to ask, but knowing she might as well. He was going to tell her, anyway. "What do you mean I owe you?"

James smiled as Will caught his fingers. "Let's just say letting me get you a cell phone will be a start toward making up for you not telling me I had a son."

Kelly's mouth dropped open as she took an egg

from the bowl. "A start? We've already been through this. I don't need a phone. This is blackmail."

He shrugged. "Maybe. Besides, a cell phone would make it easier to reach you if you're not at the clinic or home and the day care needs you."

She broke two eggs in the skillet and turned up the burner as she contemplated his words. She admitted it made sense. She'd feel better knowing they could find her if something came up with Will.

"Oh, all right, but take the money out of whatever pay I have coming."

He winked at Will, then stood. "We'll see."

"No. We will not see. If I get a phone, then I'll pay for it."

"Kel, you're—"

"I'm more than capable—"

"Kel—"

"—of taking care of me and my son. So you're wasting your breath."

"Kel, you might want to—"

She held up a hand, determined to have the last word. "I don't want to hear any more about it."

James shrugged and lifted Will from the high chair. "Fine. I'll take Will outside so the noise doesn't scare him."

"What noise?" she asked.

"When the smoke alarm goes off." James opened the back door and slipped outside as Kelly turned to the stove and the burning eggs.

A loud honking filled the kitchen. Kelly lifted the pan from the burner and set it aside. She muttered and rushed to open the door James had closed behind him, then flipped on the exhaust. Fanning a towel in the doorway, she watched James saunter across the yard with her son.

"Let's go feed the horses, Will. At least their breakfast won't be burned."

Kelly grabbed two eggs from the carton and held them behind her. "James, can you come here for a second?"

He paused, then lowered Will to the ground. Hurrying toward her, he said, "Sure, babe, what do you need?"

She drew back and threw the two eggs at him.

They splattered at his feet. He stared at the broken eggs, then grinned at her. "You burned the first ones, and I'd say these are a mite undercooked. Would you like me to fix your breakfast?"

Grabbing the skillet with the burned eggs, Kelly laughed and headed out the door, chasing after him as he caught Will and ducked into the barn.

"James Scott, you are about to get it."

She was calling a temporary halt to their truce.

James watched Will waddle bowlegged into the kitchen as if he'd been on horseback for two days without a break.

Time for a diaper change. And he would have to do it.

Kelly had gone by the day care and brought Will back to the clinic. James had brought him home while she went on a call with Cal.

And now he was going to cook her dinner. It was disgusting, but it was healthy. He stirred the liver and onions, put the lid on the pan and turned the heat control to simmer. Then he carried Will at arm's length into his bedroom where Kelly kept everything. He'd been lucky so far and hadn't had to change a dirty diaper before now, but figured it couldn't be any more difficult than a wet one. After all, he was a veterinarian who saw all kinds of questionable stuff on a daily basis.

James deposited Will in the baby bed and removed his boots and jeans. He dug around in the bag and found several alien-looking instruments before coming across a clean diaper. Taking a deep breath, he pulled the tabs and opened Will's diaper.

Oh, man. A tremor shot up his spine. He'd seen things out in the pasture that didn't look that bad. "What the devil are they feeding you at that school, anyway?"

Will smiled and rolled.

James had a lot of experience wrestling steers and caught an ankle, flipping the boy back over. "Hold on a minute, partner. Let's get you cleaned up."

Will laughed and squirmed, trying his best to work his way out from under James's hand. "Give me a break, will ya?" James grabbed the box of moist towelettes and swiped at the boy's bottom.

Will chuckled and kicked some more.

"I thought me and you were buds."

The kid thrust his legs in the air and thrashed harder.

James caught a foot and pulled Will's socks off, then tugged the shirt over his head. He carried the boy by his fingertips to the backyard. With a triumphant smile, he turned on the water and hosed off Will's backside.

The kid danced and splashed as if having the time of his life in the mud. James couldn't blame him. It smelled much better outside.

Will was fascinated by the water hose and must

have squirted everything a hundred times. Finally James carried Will into the house and stuck him in the bathtub. After Kelly called to say she was on her way home, James lifted Will from the water, ignoring his cries to stay. "I need to get supper cooked. Your mama's been working really hard at the clinic, and I want to surprise her."

Will puckered up like he was going to cry. "Mama."

"You miss her, too, huh? Well, we'll get by." James wished he knew what to do to get through to Kelly. She kept to herself as much as possible and ignored his attempts to draw her out, though he had noticed a big improvement since she'd gone to the doctor and started taking the iron supplement a week ago.

He dried Will and dressed him, then put two cans of spinach on to heat and turned the burner back up under the liver.

Though James tried to think of other things, he kept remembering the way it had been that one night between them, only Kelly didn't want that anymore. Well, he did. Surely he could figure out what to do to convince her she wanted it, too.

But how could he reach her?

The front door opened and Kelly rushed into the kitchen, scooping Will up in her arms. "Hey, what smells good?"

James lifted the lid on the skillet. "Liver and onions and spinach."

Kelly's eyes widened. "I don't remember you liking liver and onions."

"I don't," James said with a shrug, "but it's high in iron and exactly what you need. You've been working hard at the clinic, and I wanted to fix you something healthy.''

''James?''

''Yeah, babe.''

She got a sad look in her eyes. ''I don't like it, either. I had a really bad experience with a plate of liver as a kid. It makes me gag.''

He'd only wanted to help and hadn't stopped to consider that she might not like liver. ''You're kidding.''

''Since you went to all the trouble to cook it,'' she said, giving him a halfhearted grin, ''I'll try to eat some...if you'll match me bite for bite.''

James stared at the pan of liver and then glanced at Kelly. He'd wanted to help make her healthy, but no way was he eating that stuff. ''How about going out and getting a burger, fries and a shake?''

Kelly sighed. ''That sounds like heaven.''

As James put the lid on the pan and followed Kelly and Will to his truck, he knew she was wrong.

Heaven was being with her.

Chapter Seven

Kelly swatted at the offending object tickling the end of her nose. It skittered down the side of her neck.

"Mama night-night."

"Not for much longer."

She opened one eye a crack and saw Will standing beside the bed. Behind him, James grinned, twirling a feather. "You planning to sleep the whole day away?"

"It's daylight."

"It usually is when the sun's up." He glanced at his watch. "Actually it's noon."

She bolted upright in the bed. "It can't be. Noon?"

He placed a hand on her shoulder. "It's all right, Kel. It's Sunday. You don't have to go in to work today. How about a picnic?"

"A picnic? Today?"

He winked at her. "Yep."

"Where?"

"In the backyard."

"Sounds wonderful."

"You're on. Will and I are running into town to get some fried chicken and all the fixings. By the time you're showered and dressed, we'll be back. Meet us in the backyard when you're done."

He sent her a devastating smile. A jolt of excitement shot through her, reminding her of how often in the past James would do spur-of-the-moment things like this. It was one of the things she'd always loved about him.

She answered his smile with one of her own. "I can't wait."

Will climbed onto the edge of the bed and gave her a sticky kiss. James helped him down, then stood for a long moment looking at her, staring at her mouth as though he wanted to kiss her, too.

And though Kelly knew she shouldn't, she wanted it, as well.

Finally Will broke the spell by catching James's hand and jabbering something about the horses.

When the pair left, closing the door behind them, Kelly threw back the covers and hurried through her shower. Foregoing makeup, she braided her hair and donned jean shorts, a T-shirt and sneakers.

Thirty minutes later she joined them in the backyard. James had placed the sack of food in the center of a blanket spread out on the thick carpet of grass. Will's squeal from across the yard drew her gaze to her son who rode on James's wide shoulders. They stood at the corral fence, petting Matilda.

Rushing over, Kelly gave James a smile as she hugged Matilda. "I haven't been able to ride very much with school and all. I've missed it."

"I can't believe you still have this old nag."

She turned back to face him. "Like I said before,

she's family. I love her. She may not have the stamina of a younger horse, but she has heart."

Matilda nuzzled Kelly's shoulder which earned her another pat.

When Kelly turned back, she found James staring. "What? Do I have mud on my face?"

"No, just thinking how much I'd like to bury my face in your neck like Matilda, wondering what you'd do if I did."

The prospect made her temperature rise, but she didn't want to ruin his efforts to make the day enjoyable. "I'd hose you down."

The wicked gleam in his eye warned her of his intent. She squealed and ran.

James took off after her, not really trying to catch her, because he still had Will on his shoulders. But he zigged and zagged across the yard, making their son giggle with delight. After fifteen minutes of playing cat and mouse, Kelly tumbled onto the blanket, ready to eat.

While James unloaded the food cartons, she cleaned Will's face and hands. Then they dined on fried chicken and corn on the cob, which turned out to be Will's favorite.

"So, how does it feel to be so close to achieving your dream?" he asked.

"I won't believe it until I have that diploma in my hand. I've had too many dreams evaporate to get my hopes up."

James paused in his chewing to study her. "Such as?"

"Oh, nothing much," she said with a shrug. "Just childhood stuff."

"Like hoping your sister would grow a wart on the end of her nose or your brother would lose his hair."

She smiled at his teasing. "No, nothing like that."

"You know, Kel, you've never said anything about your family. I don't even know if you have a sister or brother."

"There's nothing to tell." She made the mistake of looking into his eyes and felt herself becoming lost in them.

She was thankful that just then Will finished eating and wanted to play with the water hose. James turned the faucet on low for Will while Kelly lay back, watching the cloud formations overhead, thankful for the reprieve.

Finishing his drink, James kicked off his boots and settled beside her.

Kelly looked at his bare feet. She would give anything to be as spontaneous as him. As it was, the only time she came close to doing anything impetuous was when she was with him.

"James, I want to thank you for letting me stay here with you. Seems like you're always having to pull my tail out of the fire," she said, plucking a blade of grass and rolling to her side to tickle James's ear.

He made a grab for her hand with the offending weapon. "Hey, you've done the same for me on several occasions."

"We've had a lot of fun together, a lot of close calls, too."

"Yeah, that's for sure." James looked toward Will. "That's far enough, buddy. Come back over this direction." He wiggled his toes. "Man, this is great. Growing up, we were never allowed to go barefoot.

My mother had this thing about us keeping our shoes on.''

"There were times I went barefoot because I didn't have shoes.''

He turned to stare at her. "What do you mean?''

Kelly realized she'd revealed too much. "Just lean times when money was tight.''

"I guess all families go through that." James rolled onto his back. "How many times in the past have we laid back like this, Kel, staring up at the Texas sky, whiling away the hours as if nothing else mattered?''

Thirty-five. "Too many to count.''

"Do you remember the score?''

"It's 204 to 198.''

"My favor?''

"Nope," Kelly answered, looking at where Will was spraying water on a rock beside them.

James pointed upward. "Look, there's Matilda.''

She strained to see. "Where?''

He scooted closer until their heads met. "Right there, next to the huge cloud mass. At about eleven o'clock.''

Kelly rolled to face him. "No way. She is not *that* swayback.''

He turned toward her. "Babe, I hate to tell you, but she is.''

"I know, but I still love her.''

"And that's what I like most about you, always looking for the good things. Somehow you always managed to find something good in me, at least before. And now it's 204 to 199." He brushed his lips against hers, then withdrew slightly, looking as surprised as she felt at his actions. After a long, lingering look, he kissed her again, his lips gentle against hers. The slight pressure of his mouth caused a flood of emotions to rise within her. It was a kiss born of need, but not a physical need. This kiss was different. It almost bordered on desperation.

Kelly slipped her arms around him, knowing she shouldn't. But she could no more stop the action than she could lasso the clouds. What could it hurt to let him hold her, just this once?

She heard Will giggle, then felt the water raining down on them.

James scrambled to his feet, catching Will as his short legs pumped to run away.

Kelly laughed so hard she settled back on the blanket, content to watch father and son, the two loves of her life, bond.

The familiar scent of sweaty animals and hay came to Kelly as she nodded at familiar faces on her way to the back of the Fort Worth coliseum.

She had left Will at home with James for the evening and had run into town to do some shopping. On the way she'd discovered Cal had gone out to the rodeo on an emergency run for a mare who had cut herself and she had swung by to see if he needed a hand.

"And now you're in for a real treat, folks," the announcer said, his voice echoing inside the coliseum. "These boys are the last contestants in team roping. Shorty Green's partner had to leave to take his son to the hospital, but a cowboy who won the coveted title of best-all-around cowboy a couple of years ago volunteered to ride header for Shorty. Let's hear a round of applause for Shorty Green and James Scott."

Kelly's steps faltered as she turned toward the

chutes. She recognized James, sitting tall in the saddle, his hat pulled low, his rope coiled and ready. She glanced around, wondering who had Will.

She heard the clatter of the metal cage as a steer was released, then the roar of the crowd, and knew James's rope had hit its mark around the steer's neck. A second roar that sent the crowd to its feet indicated Shorty's rope had ensnared both hind feet.

Climbing up on the bottom rung of a chute, she looked out over the crowd, hoping to see her son. Nothing. She jumped down and hurried toward the spot behind the chutes where James would leave the arena.

"Well," the announcer said, "let's see what the clock says. Six point five zero. That means Shorty and James are our winners tonight."

Kelly pushed through the crowd, fear and anger raging inside her. Had James brought Will out here? She hoped not. An accident could happen around an animal in the blink of an eye. *Please, God, let Will be safe.*

By the time she reached James, he was surrounded by buckle bunnies and cowboys. Her heart thundered in her chest. "Where is Will?"

"He's all right," James said, catching her arm. "I left him with Sara to come out here to help Cal with that emergency."

"Thank goodness." She glanced around him to the horse he'd just dismounted. "Is that the emergency?"

"You know it's not. Cal said he could handle stitching the injured horse, and Shorty needed a partner. It was no big deal."

"It is a big deal." She couldn't seem to stop the anger and feelings of desertion. It was like a snowball effect. Only, she didn't know where it came from, just that it had her firmly in its grip. "Did you really do it for your friend? Or is it the thrill you get, the thrill you need?"

James pulled her through the crowd toward the double doors leading outside. "I had no intention of riding when I came out here. When Cal took the call he thought the gash might require stitches inside and out and asked if I'd meet him. Then Marty's kid got hurt and they took him to the E.R. After Cal told me he could handle the call himself, I volunteered to be Shorty's partner so he wouldn't lose his entry fee. You would have done the same."

"No, I wouldn't. If you really want to be Will's father, then you need to remember you have a son and quit putting everybody else first."

Something akin to hurt flashed in his eyes, then was gone, leaving her wondering if it had been a trick of the lighting. "Dammit, I know I have a son. This is the first time I've ridden in a month, and it wasn't planned."

When Kelly had first come back, she'd actually seen signs that James might be different now. She certainly hadn't expected him to change because of her but had hoped he might for his son. "What are you going to do when Will gets older and does something on a whim, something you're not happy about?"

"Depending on what it is, I'll talk to him. You're just ticked because my being here wasn't on one of your lists or schedules."

She wished the knot in her stomach would ease. "You know I came back here so you could spend time with Will, but here you are off chasing rainbows. What am I supposed to think?"

James's eyes darkened. All traces of emotion disappeared, except the hard set of his jaw. "I don't know, Kelly. You quit listening to me a long time ago. I want Will to grow up, knowing the bond of friendship. That means helping each other when necessary, giving as well as taking. I think that's a lesson you could stand to learn."

Kelly clung tight to her control. She sucked in the night air, willing her frazzled nerves to calm.

"What's going on, Kel?" James frowned at her, his eyes cold and hard, sending a tremor down her spine. "I don't think you're really mad because I have friends."

Kelly couldn't speak for the loneliness that filled her. She tried to resurrect the indifference she'd shown during those times as a child when she'd been returned to the foster care system by couples who'd promised to love her forever. Only, it didn't ease her pain as it had then. Maybe that was because now she knew better than to believe in miracles or to count on anyone except herself.

James cupped her chin, forcing her to look at him, as a calf bawled in the distance. "Don't you know I left Will with Sara so he wouldn't be in danger? Marty's boy was kicked by a horse and had to have stitches. I don't think I could stand it if that happened to Will. If I'd had him with me, I would never have gotten on that horse. Dammit, Kelly, I love him."

His admission caught her off guard. She hadn't expected him to have feelings for Will until later in the summer, *after* he'd spent more time with him.

Though she'd learned long ago that saying something didn't necessarily make it so, she wanted to believe James. More than one set of prospective parents had promised to love her forever. But they hadn't. She never wanted Will to know that kind of hurt, and she clung to the hope that James meant what he'd said.

In the past she had always relied on him. She still did. As hard as it was for her to admit, he was being a responsible father by not having Will out here where he would be in danger. It was only her own insecurities where James was concerned that were standing in the way now.

"Let's go get Will and go home," James said, placing his hand at her elbow.

"Shouldn't we check with Cal before we leave?"

"I talked to him right before I rode. He had it under control. You and I need to sit down and have a long talk."

"It won't change my mind. I meant what I said about Will. I don't want him left standing on the sidelines waiting for you to finish doing favors for your friends. He deserves more. He deserves quality time."

"I agree he does. But you're judging me based on some preconceived notion of what you think I am, and, honey, I hate to tell you, but you're wrong."

She sighed. "James, I found you out here getting off a horse. What am I supposed to think?"

"That I'd done something honorable and good. I was just leaving to go get Will."

Kelly stared at James, too tired to make sense of anything.

A cowboy hurried by, a coiled rope in one hand. "Good ride." He paused to eye Kelly, then punched James's shoulder and winked. "Now I see why you were in an all-fired hurry to leave."

As the man rushed inside, Kelly asked, "What was that all about?"

"Jed had asked me to go throw back a few cold ones tonight. I turned him down."

"Why?"

James shrugged. "I didn't want to leave Will with Sara for too long." He glanced at his watch. "If I leave now, I can get him home so that he's in bed on schedule."

"You told me that you don't ride very often," she said, feeling less angry and now somewhat guilty for overreacting. "I never stopped to think what having us around might do to your life, your rodeoing."

James toed the ground with a booted foot. "Your being here hasn't caused me any problem. I haven't competed seriously for quite a while."

Now that she thought about it, he hadn't ridden or gone near the rodeo since her return over a month ago. She'd been pretty tough on him just now and wondered what else she'd been wrong about. "James, I'm sorry. I was wrong to jump you like that. I've had a rough day and I'm tired."

"Don't worry about it."

When he leaned forward as if to kiss her, Kelly took a step back. "I'd better go get Will." She hurried to her truck and climbed inside, calling herself a coward, then sat in the dark for a while. Had James been right? She didn't know what to believe. She'd made so many mistakes where he was concerned.

They'd been friends before they'd been lovers. And he'd helped her with things, same as he'd done tonight for Marty. She'd had no right to get angry with him. Sure, she had been worried about Will, but that didn't excuse what she'd done.

Tonight when she got home, she would apologize again. From now on she'd think before she opened her mouth, because she had never been any good at eating crow.

The next evening James handed Will a bowl of macaroni and cheese as Kelly bounced into the kitchen.

She wore a pair of cutoff jean shorts and an oversize T-shirt that hid more than it revealed. Her hair was twisted into a weird knot of sorts behind her head, and she was barefoot.

When Kelly saw he'd cooked while she'd showered, she skidded to a stop. "Oh, boy. Should I get excited? Are we having liver and onions again?" The smile that broke through before she giggled illuminated the kitchen.

James had never wanted her more than he did at this moment.

He gave her a playful scowl to let her know he didn't appreciate her taunt. "No, Miss Smarty Pants. I stopped on my way home from that last call and picked up barbecue and all the trimmings. I seem to recall you like barbecue."

Her eyes lit up and she licked her bottom lip. "Oh, yum. I'm starved."

The urge to draw her into his arms and hold her tight shook him. Instead, he retrieved the spoon Will had thrown on the floor and tossed it in the sink.

"I have it on good authority that Smoky's barbecue is better than liver and onions for building iron."

Kelly almost skipped over to the counter where he'd opened the cartons. She closed her eyes and inhaled the spicy fragrance. "I'm sure that's probably true, because no matter how much iron the food contains, it doesn't do any good if you don't eat it."

After she had filled a plate and taken a seat at the table, he straddled a chair next to Will. James wished he could make her understand his concern for her future, though he wasn't entirely sure he understood. Last night she'd made it clear she still thought him irresponsible and hadn't given him a real chance to prove otherwise. He was found guilty without the benefit of a trial. From the day she'd returned he'd felt as if he'd been stuck on an out-of-control roller coaster with no way off. "I hate the thought of you going back to school and wearing yourself out. Have you considered cutting back on the courses you're taking?"

She pushed a bite of potato salad around her plate. "I've always wanted to be a vet. I love working with horses. I really do want to go back to school and finish, but Will is the most important thing. I pushed myself last year. Being here with you and Will has made me realize what a destructive pattern I'd fallen into. Thinking I was really sick was a wake-up call. I can't do that again."

"What can I do to help?"

Their eyes met and held. "You've already done far more than I ever could have expected. You've helped me see what's important in life—and that's being with Will. Next time it might not be anemia. If something should ever happen to me, I want him to remember more than just that his mom was driven to succeed."

James stood and poured milk into a clown cup, then added a spoon of chocolate powder before screwing on the lid. "I wish the college were closer. I worry about you and him."

She frowned. "You don't need to, you know. I'm glad we came here and that Will had this time with you, but I don't want you to be concerned. We're both okay."

He settled the cup on Will's high chair tray and ruffled his hair. "Your mama is obstinate."

Will nodded and pointed toward Kelly. "Mama."

James cocked a hip against the counter and crossed one booted ankle over the other. He didn't want to think about them leaving. He wanted to be with his son all the time. And seeing Kelly returning to her old self, full of spit and vinegar, made him want to kiss her. And if he did, it wouldn't be a kiss between friends.

He needed to get away from her to regain control, so he headed for the back door. "I'll be back in a minute. I'm going to feed the horses."

"Horsey go," Will shouted, and squirmed in the high chair, doing his best to get out. "Daddy, go," he yelled again.

Kelly gasped. Her fork clattered against her plate.

James froze. His gut tightened into a hard knot, then eased as pride filled him.

"I hadn't thought Will would know to call you that," Kelly said, concern in her eyes.

"That's what I am, Kel. When it's just the two of us doing things together, I'm Daddy. That's what I started calling myself to him. It's Daddy who takes him outside and Daddy who takes him to feed the horses. I admit I had hoped he might say it, but he hasn't until now."

"I was just surprised to hear him call you that."

James crossed the room and slid the tray out, then lifted Will. "Why? That's what I am."

"I know. It just caught me off guard is all. I know

it's foolish, but for a second there I felt threatened, as if I was losing Will to you, and I know that's absurd.''

James hadn't realized until now how Kelly might feel. She'd had the boy all to herself for two years. Now she was having to share him. He supposed under the circumstances, he could sympathize. ''Just because Will called me Daddy doesn't mean he loves you any less.''

''I know, and I'm really glad Will has had this chance to get to know you. I just don't want him hurt.''

''What do you mean?''

''Every day he grows more attached to you. And that's good. It's why I came back.''

''But?''

Kelly's gaze locked with his. ''What about after I return to school, next month, next year? Will you really be there for him?''

''No one ever knows what the future holds in store, but, yeah, I intend to be a part of his life. If I could, I'd be there for him every minute of every day.''

She watched him, her shoulders slumping as if in relief. ''I just don't want Will ever to feel caught in the middle between us. I want him to be happy, and I think he can be so long as we remain friends.''

When Will wriggled, James lowered him to the floor. ''Is being friends what you really want?''

''Of course,'' she said, unable to meet his eyes. ''What else is there?''

''You and me and what's between us.''

Kelly inhaled sharply. ''What are you saying?''

''I don't want to be your friend anymore.''

''What do you mean?'' she asked.

What *did* he mean? ''I don't know,'' he answered.

"Marriage?"

James stared at her. "Not exactly."

She laughed, but it was a nervous sound without humor. "Thank goodness. You scared me there for a minute. So if not marriage, then what?"

"I don't know. I just keep thinking about what happened between us before you left."

She chewed her bottom lip. "You mean *that* night?"

If he hadn't been so tense, he would have laughed. The way she'd referred to what had happened between them sounded as if it had been a national disaster rather than two people making love. "Yeah, Kel. That's what I mean."

"I don't think that's a good idea. If it didn't work out, then Will would be the one to suffer. I have to go back to school. And apparently your rodeoing still means a lot to you."

He didn't understand why she obviously still had such a problem with him competing every now and then. Rodeoing was an honorable sport, something to be proud of. There were a lot of father-and-son teams on the circuit. And it was hard work and required a lot of talent and dedication.

Maybe if he kept reasoning with her, Kelly would get over it. He smiled at the stubborn set of her jaw. Then again, maybe not. "Maybe we should give it a try, see what happens."

"James, I really think we'd be asking for trouble. Look at last night. I mean, I'm sorry about the way I acted." She frowned. "Okay, I admit I overreacted. I know I was wrong, but I didn't know where Will was. I was really scared."

"There are always going to be times when we don't agree."

"But if we aren't able to work it out, that puts Will in the middle of a difficult situation." She picked Will up and held him close. "I need to give Will a bath."

He watched her hurry from the kitchen, wondering if they would ever have an entire conversation before she found some excuse to run off.

He suddenly remembered the *M* word she'd used. Marriage.

The idea of living the way he did now, with Kelly and Will, but with her sharing his bed every night and waking up every morning with her in his arms didn't scare him nearly as much as it might have a few years ago.

But if they were married, she would expect more. She'd expect him to live by her danged rules.

And that was something he had never been able to do.

Chapter Eight

Kelly jumped from her pickup the following morning and leaned against the front fender while waiting on Cal. They were going to check on Spencer Jefferson's new colt.

She couldn't get yesterday's conversation with James out of her mind. His suggestion that they go back to what they'd once shared had surprised her. Even more surprising was she'd been tempted.

Living with James permanently was out of the question. It wouldn't be a good example for Will. Even if their relationship remained strictly platonic, people talked. While she didn't give a hoot what others thought, she didn't want Will hurt by idle gossip. Who knew what damage had already been done?

The front door opened and Cal walked down the porch steps and across the yard, followed by Sara with Jessie on her hip.

Kelly smiled at Jessie and leaned forward to touch

the golden curls glistening in the morning sun. "She's a doll. You must be so proud of her."

Sara beamed with pride. "Yes, and I've noticed James feels the same about Will. He's really good with kids."

"James is Jessie's godfather," Cal said.

"You'd trust him to raise Jessie? What about him rodeoing?" Kelly asked, surprised she'd voiced her concerns.

Cal gave Kelly a questioning look. "He has a good heart. I know he'd do whatever it took to take care of my child."

When Cal kissed Jessie and Sara goodbye, Kelly moved toward his truck. She knew that James was a good man. Cal and Sara had no doubts about James caring for their child. And he had certainly been good to her and Will since she'd come back.

When Cal caught up with her, Kelly asked, "What's on the agenda for today?"

"First is checking Jefferson's new colt, then old man Duffy wants us to take a look at his herd. It may be a long day."

Kelly clipped the cell phone James had insisted she carry on her belt.

Cal opened the door to his truck. "One other thing. James went through a lot after you left. I don't want to know what's going on between you two. But I hope that before you turn your back on him again, make sure you know what you're throwing away, for yourself and Will."

She had searched her entire life for someone to love her and thought maybe she'd found him in James, but then she'd sacrificed everything for one night in his arms.

And her world had crumbled.

Now, after hearing the things Cal and Sara had said, she had to wonder if she'd allowed past hurts to blind her to the real man behind the chaps.

James checked the foreleg of the horse. The new treatment he'd used had paid off. If it had failed, he would more than likely have lost a good client and could possibly be facing a lawsuit. Yeah, he'd been lucky.

Too bad his good fortune didn't extend to Kelly. He was at a loss as to what to do where she was concerned. He admired her veterinary skills and admitted she would likely make a name for herself in the equine community. He just wished she didn't have to leave to go back to school. Not that he would ever ask her to give up her dreams. But he could ask her to relocate. That wouldn't be the same thing as making a commitment.

Pleased with the horse's progress, James left the stall and washed his hands. The phone rang, and he caught it on the third ring. "C-J Equine Clinic."

"Kelly Mathews, please."

"Kelly's not here right now. Can I have her call you?"

"Oh, dear," the woman said, concern evident in her voice.

"Is there a problem?"

"Well, yes. This is Mrs. Grayson from Miss Clancy's Little People. Do you know where we can reach Ms. Mathews?"

"What's wrong?" he asked, his hold on the receiver tightening along with his gut.

"I'm sorry, but I'm not allowed to divulge any information regarding her child to anyone other than Ms. Mathews.''

"This is James Scott—Dr. James Scott. I'm Will's father. You can tell me.''

"Well, I don't know. I don't see your name listed on the contact sheet.''

"Lady, you can take my word for it. I'm Will's father. Now, what's wrong?''

Obviously flustered, Mrs. Grayson said, "Could you get a message to Ms. Mathews?''

"Of course,'' James snapped, his patience at an end.

A sigh of relief came through the phone. "Tell her to come get her son as soon as possible.''

"Why?''

"He's ill,'' Mrs. Grayson said.

"He was fine this morning. What seems to be the problem?''

"I guess it's okay to tell you since you'll find the child's mother. The boy is running a fever.''

James had been around Cal and Sara's baby, Jessie, enough to know fever in a kid wasn't a good thing. "How high a fever?''

"I assure you that we're very competent. The children had been outside playing. When we realized that Will was running a fever and not just hot from playing, well, it was already pretty high.''

James frowned. The concern in the woman's voice worried him. "How high?''

"One hundred four. Since high fever can be dangerous, I think Ms. Mathews should take him straight to the doctor.''

"I'll be right there.''

"Oh, but you're not on the list.''

"Lady, hang your list.'' James hung up and headed

out the door toward his truck. Once on the road, he dialed the number for the phone he'd bought Kelly. He knew she'd gone to help Cal on several jobs today. After ringing three times, her voice mail kicked in, and he left a message that Will was sick. He tried calling Sara at home and, getting no answer, he tried Cal's cell phone. He left a message at both places.

He tried several more times to reach Kelly as he drove into town, wishing he'd pinned her down earlier and gotten a list of where she planned to be and at what times. Twenty minutes later he parked in front of Miss Clancy's Little People and hurried inside. He stooped to talk to a young woman in a glassed-in cage. "I'm James Scott. I'm here to pick up my son, Will Scott. Can you tell me where he is?"

She smiled at him. "I'm sorry, but we don't have a Will Scott. Do you have the right day care?"

James frowned. "Someone just called from here and said Will's sick."

"Oh, you mean Will Mathews."

"Mathews?" Kelly's maiden name. James's gut knotted with hurt and confusion. Why had she not given their son the name Scott? Will deserved to bear that name. It was his birthright, his heritage. This was one time he intended to make Kelly listen to reason. But first he had to see to his son.

The secretary directed James to a room down the hall. He hurried through the doorway into an open room where children played. One woman sat in a corner away from everyone, rocking Will.

James crossed the room in five steps and scooped his son in his arms. The boy's listlessness scared him. Without a word to the woman who'd been holding Will, James hurried from the building.

As he reached his truck, an older lady caught up with him. "Sir, I cannot permit you to take the boy. You're not on our list."

"Look, I'm Will's father. I'm sure it's just a mistake. I'm taking him to the doctor."

"I cannot release Will to you until I receive verification from Ms. Mathews."

"Will is sick. I'm taking him to the doctor."

Her spine stiffened. "If you leave with the child, I'll have no alternative but to call the police."

"Then you'd better start dialing, because I'm taking him." James buckled Will in his car seat and hurried around the truck. Sliding behind the wheel, he glanced at the old woman who stood on the sidewalk wringing her hands. He wondered if she really would call the police and hoped that if she did, they wouldn't stop him until after he'd gotten Will to the doctor.

He started his pickup and backed out. Unsure if Kelly had a preference for doctors, he decided to take Will to the same doctor Sara used for Jessie. James had been out to the man's home a couple of times to treat his horses and was impressed by the care the doctor gave his stock.

As he drove to the doctor's office, he pressed his fingers against Will's forehead, and the tightness in his chest grew worse.

Once he got Will taken care of, he'd find out why Kelly hadn't seen fit to give his last name to his son.

James left another message on Kelly's cell phone, telling her where to find him, then parked in the clinic parking lot. He hurried around the truck and lifted Will in his arms. The boy's skin burned him where they touched, and he swallowed past the sudden constriction in his throat.

He carried Will inside to the reception desk. "I need to see Dr. Parker."

A woman behind the counter looked over the top of her glasses at him. "Do you have an appointment?"

"No."

"Then you'll have to make one and come back."

"I can't. My son's running a fever. He needs to be seen now."

The woman clicked the mouse and stared at the computer screen. "We're booked solid today. We do have an opening tomorrow afternoon. Your name, please."

"Where's Dr. Parker?"

"He's with a patient. Now, if you'll give me your name."

James carried Will to the end of the counter where he saw a door. He assumed it led to the examining rooms.

The woman pushed her chair back, but didn't reach him before he'd gone through the door. "Sir, you can't go back there."

"The hell I can't. Where's Dr. Parker?"

Another nurse, this one younger, hurried from one of the patient rooms. "Is there a problem here?"

James paused. "Yeah, my boy's burning up with fever, and I need to find Dr. Parker."

Her gaze dropped to Will's flushed face. "Follow me."

The old bat behind him muttered as she retraced her steps.

The nurse indicated a room, and James kicked the door open. She lined the examination table with fresh paper. "Put him there and take his clothes off. I need to take his temperature."

James lowered Will to the paper and tried with shaky fingers to undo the buttons on his shirt.

The nurse nudged him aside and removed Will's shirt, boots and jeans. When she inserted a funny-looking gadget in Will's ear, James asked, "Don't you need to get the doctor?"

"Yes, but I need to know what his temperature is first." A moment later the instrument beeped, and she looked at the digital display.

"Well?" James asked.

"Stick your head out that door and ask a nurse to get Dr. Parker. I need to get this baby's fever down."

Without a word of argument, James hurried into the hallway and grabbed the first woman he saw dressed in white. "We need Dr. Parker in that room right now. Can you get him?"

She stared up at him, her eyes wide, but finally nodded.

James raced back to his son, feeling about as helpless as he'd ever felt.

The nurse had wet a cloth and was wiping Will down. "Here, do this while I get another one."

He took the rag she handed him and ran it up Will's chest. Everywhere he touched burned him. Fear lodged in his chest.

Dr. Parker hurried into the room, acknowledging James with a nod. He had barely exchanged a few words with the nurse when two police officers burst into the room.

The oldest of the pair approached James. "You James Scott?"

James exhaled a slow breath. "Yeah."

He indicated Will. "That the boy you took from the day care?"

"Yes. He's my son."

Dr. Parker interrupted their conversation. "Excuse me, but you're going to have to take care of this outside."

"I'm not leaving my boy."

"I can't treat your son with all of you in here arguing. Go outside so I can do my job."

With some reluctance James followed the policemen into the hallway, but he dug in his heels when they tried to go farther. "I'm not moving from this spot until I know how my son's doing."

"I understand. I'm a father, too." The officer opened a notepad and withdrew a pen from his shirt pocket. "Now, show me some identification and tell me what happened."

James pulled his license from his wallet and recited the morning's events, starting with the phone call from the school.

"Where's Will? What's happened?"

He turned to find Kelly rushing toward him.

Without caring what the police thought, James caught her in his arms and held her tight. From her lack of color and the way she shook, she needed him right now.

And damned if he didn't need her, too.

Kelly leaned into James, needing his strength. But more than that, she needed to find out about her son. "Where's Will?" Then she noticed the policemen, and her knees buckled. "Oh, no. What's happened to him?"

James caught her elbow before she hit the floor and

pulled her back to her feet. He wiped the tears from her cheek. "The doctor is with Will right now."

"Then why are the police here?"

"Mrs. Grayson at the day care called about Will. She said he was sick, so I went to get him. But when I took him from the school, she called the police."

Kelly's eyes widened. "I don't understand. Why would she do that?"

"Because you didn't put me on the list as Will's dad."

She took a step back. "It never occurred to me you'd ever need to pick him up."

The officer stepped forward. "You're the boy's mother?"

"Yes."

"Your name, please."

"Kelly Mathews."

"Is Mr. Scott the child's father?"

She glanced from the officer to James. "Yes. Yes, he is."

"I assume then you won't want to press kidnapping charges against him."

"No, of course not." She swallowed as she noticed the concern in James's eyes when he glanced at the door behind her.

"I guess that's all. Thank you. We'll leave you two to see about your son," the older policeman said, then he and his partner left as the door to the examining room opened.

James rushed forward, settling his arm over Kelly's shoulders. He propelled her into the room, and they faced the doctor together.

"What is it?" James asked.

"An ear and throat infection," he said. "Has he run a fever like this before?"

"No," Kelly said, needing to hold her child. "Will's never sick."

"I'll give you a prescription for an antibiotic," the doctor said as he scribbled in a chart. "Do you have something at home to give him for his fever? I've given him some medicine already, but his temperature may spike again during the night. I suggest you get up throughout the night to check him. If he's not better by tomorrow or if his fever doesn't go down, give me a call."

The doctor shook James's hand, then slipped outside, along with the nurse.

Kelly stared at her baby, who whimpered upon seeing her. Tears filled her eyes as she watched Will, so tiny and helpless, lying on the table. She worked her hands beneath him and lifted him against her heart. He'd needed her and she hadn't been there. She'd done the one thing she'd sworn to never do. She'd failed him.

Only then did she realize Will was trying to lean away from her, holding his arms out to James.

Though she wanted to hold Will tight as if that would keep him from further harm, she allowed James to take him. Watching her son press his head into the crook of his father's neck almost sent Kelly to her knees. When James closed his eyes and hugged his son, then pressed a kiss against the top of his head, she felt like an outsider intruding on a private moment.

The sudden weakness in her knees forced her into a chair. The fact that Will had chosen James over her didn't mean he didn't love her, too. Will would be all right. That's all that mattered.

"I thought it was going to be something awful," James said, moving to the table to finish dressing Will. "It never occurred to me that an ear infection could make him this sick."

She clenched her eyes shut against the tears that scalded her eyes, not ready to voice her own failure.

James moved to her side, Will in his arms, and frowned. "Kel, you all right? What's wrong?"

Tears dripped from her chin. "My baby needed me, and I wasn't there for him. What kind of mother am I?"

He pulled Kelly to her feet and used the pads of his thumbs to wipe the dampness from her cheeks. "Shh. You're a good mother. None of this was your fault."

"Yes, it was."

"No, hon, it wasn't." James put one arm around her shoulders and held her tight, then pressed a gentle kiss against her forehead.

Kelly didn't want to need him, to want him, but she did. Having no strength left to fight him after what had happened to her son, she leaned into James, allowing him to soothe her worries. Just for a minute.

His free hand stroked her back, easing her tension with his gentle touch. Still, she fretted over what could have happened if James hadn't been there, if he hadn't taken charge.

The door behind them opened, and Kelly stepped back.

The nurse smiled at James and handed him the prescription. "You should get this filled when you leave here. Give your son a dose as soon as you get home and then every four hours after that."

James took the paper. "Thanks for your help. We appreciate it."

He relinquished Will to Kelly as they headed out to pay the bill.

Kelly remembered the times as a child when she'd been sick, how she'd longed for someone to hold her close, to care. It broke her heart to think her son might have cried for her, and she hadn't been there.

But James had.

James tiptoed into the room behind Kelly and paused at the edge of Will's crib. He leaned around her to press the backs of his fingers to Will's cheek. His son was cooler to the touch now, his temperature having dropped within an hour of taking the medicine, as the doctor had predicted.

Still, James couldn't help but worry about a recurrence. "You told the doctor Will's never been this sick before."

"Will's like you, always on the go. He's too busy to be sick."

"I've seen Jessie when she's had a cold, but never anything as scary as this."

"High fever is nothing to mess around with." She yawned. "I hope Will's never ill like this again. I feel like I've been through the wringer."

Knowing he probably shouldn't, James turned Kelly to face him and pulled her into his arms. "It's been a tough day. I'll call the doctor tomorrow and find out if we should take Will to a specialist to have his ears checked."

Kelly yawned again and nuzzled her cheek against his chest. "Some kids get ear infections a lot. I think I've been very fortunate that Will has been as healthy as he has. Since this is his only ear infection, I doubt they'll think it necessary for him to see a specialist."

This was the first time he'd held Kelly when she didn't resist. It felt so good. This was something he could get used to, not that Kelly would let him, since she still insisted they be friends. "You know so much more about kids than I do," James said, again realizing how much he'd missed by not being a part of Will's childhood.

She shrugged. "I've had him for two years. You pick stuff up over time. By tomorrow he'll probably be back to his old self."

"I don't think I'll ever be the same." The fear he'd experienced when he'd seen Will so out of it would stay with him the rest of his life, the same as the sense of loss he'd felt after Kelly had left.

"Once school starts and we leave, things will get back to normal for you."

"Do you really think that after being together every day for three months, you and Will can walk out of my life, and I'll not even notice you're gone?"

Kelly drew back, eyes wide. "I'm sorry. That's not exactly what I meant."

"I might have felt that way before you left, but this is now. And Will is my son. I care a great deal for him...and you. You moving to A&M won't change how I feel." He couldn't imagine his life without the boy. Or Kelly. No matter her plans, he intended to be a part of his son's life. Hers, too, if she would only let him. "Have you given any thought to relocating?"

She lifted her chin, and their gazes met briefly. "What do you mean?"

"Finding a college closer."

"You know as well as I do there's only one in this state that offers a degree in veterinary medicine," she said.

"I know that. I guess I'm not thinking straight. I know you have a life schedule and want to finish school, but don't forget there's more to life than getting a degree and accomplishing goals."

"I know that, James," she said, a wistful quality to her voice. "You taught me that years ago, but with the hustle and bustle of school, I'd forgotten. Being here with you has reminded me of that."

His eyes never left hers. He couldn't understand the sadness he saw there. "You won't consider relocating?"

She placed her hand on his arm. "I wish I could. I know being with you is something Will needs, but I think being on the road all the time would make it harder on me to keep up with my studies. I know you understand my reasoning."

"I do, but I want to be with Will. The farther away you are, the harder it will be."

She removed her hand from his and turned to stare at their sleeping son for a long while. "I don't know exactly how to answer that." She paused as if stalling for time to find the right words. "I want you to see Will anytime you want, but after graduation I don't know where I'll go. It just depends on what jobs are available. You being able to see him whenever you want may not always be possible, depending on where I end up."

James wasn't thrilled to hear that. "Kel, I'll do whatever it takes to see Will. I've driven from one side of the country to the other with little or no sleep following rodeos. No matter where you go, I'll be there for Will." *And for you.*

"I don't want you to feel obligated though, James."

"Obligated? He's my son. I am obligated."

"What I was trying to say was *trapped*. You didn't ask for all of this, and I don't want you to feel trapped."

"I don't." James realized then that he didn't feel trapped. He never had. What he felt was frustration that he couldn't get Kelly to face some things. "The other night I mentioned us going back to what we had before—"

"Look, James, I'm not sure, I don't think—"

"Why not?" he asked.

"That's not my idea of being a family. I don't think living together would work."

"It's been working," he said, cupping her shoulders with his palms.

She flinched at the force of his words. "Being friends is not the same thing as living together, and you know it."

"You're hedging."

"I don't know what you want me to say." Kelly backed away from his touch and stared at the floor. "I think we're better off as friends. I think it's what's best for Will."

He cupped her chin. "Look at me."

Kelly allowed him to tip her head back. "All right. I'm looking."

"We're good together." He watched shadows from the lamp dance on her face as he ran his thumb across her cheek.

"Do you mean in bed?"

He smiled, then shrugged. "Well, I wasn't going to bring that up, but I suppose since you did, that's as good a place as any to start."

"You know, James," she said, giving him a look

of exasperation, "you are making me crazy. *That* happened three years ago. And look at what came of it."

He ran his fingertips down the curve of her jaw. "Yeah. A beautiful son."

She smiled. "You're right. I can't deny that."

"Aside from Will, can't you feel what's between us?" he asked, pulling her closer, framing her face in his hands. "It's more than just friendship."

"We tried it before. It didn't work." Her words wobbled. She breathed hard as if she'd run a race.

"You didn't give it a chance. We get along great. We haven't argued...much. Why wouldn't it work?"

"Because, because... I don't know why. It just wouldn't."

He kissed her forehead, her temple and then her ear.

Kelly pressed her palms against his chest and stepped back. "We're friends. And friends don't kiss."

The doubt he saw in her eyes convinced him she didn't quite believe everything she said. James's hand circled her neck, reining her in. He brushed his mouth over hers, then nibbled her lower lip. "This friend does."

Kelly groaned when her arms wound around his neck as he trailed kisses down hers. "We can't live together, not like that."

"Why?" James straightened and cocked his head back to look at her. He wondered how long it would take her to face the truth.

"We're great friends. I'm happy with that."

He kissed her, then pulled away only far enough to whisper, "No, you're not. And I can prove it." He caught her hips and walked her backward until she was against the wall. He leaned into her, leaving no doubt about how much he wanted her.

"You've been here for ten weeks and I haven't done a single thing out of line, except for a few kisses. Not that I didn't want to. I've taken more cold showers than any man ought to have to endure just so I could keep my damned hands off you. And do you know why?"

She shook her head, her eyes wide.

"Because I wanted you to see there's more to me than just a roll in the hay, that I'm dependable, responsible. But you won't let go of your stupid rules long enough to give me a chance. Well, I'm tired of talking. I'm tired of being patient, waiting on you to see what's so danged obvious. Nothing I've tried has worked. And every time I do something that makes you wonder if maybe you might be wrong about me, you make up another damned rule. I only know one other way to reach you, one other thing I haven't tried. And that's to kiss you until you can't think. Maybe then you'll listen to me."

She didn't resist when he tugged her close, molding her body to his. "James, please—"

"Please what?" His hands skittered over her curves. He longed to hear her admit what he already knew. "Tell me want what we had before. Dammit, Kel, you're driving me wild with needing you."

When his mouth covered hers, she tilted her head to deepen the kiss, catching his hair to pull him closer as she arched against him.

"Tell me we're not good together," he said against her lips. "Tell me we couldn't make it work."

Her eyes shot open, her blue gaze burning him. She used the wall as leverage and gave him a hard shove.

"Blast you, James. I can't believe you'd stoop so low as to try to seduce me, to use my weakness for you against me, just to get your way."

"Weakness," he said with a slow grin, letting his hands drop to his sides. "I didn't know I had that effect on you."

"Why are you asking me this now?"

"Because I want you and my son. And, dammit, I want Will to bear my name."

She gasped. "When did you find out?"

"When I went to pick him up at the day care."

"So, you'd saddle yourself with me just to put your label on Will?"

"You're twisting my words."

"I don't think so. You don't have to put up with me to change Will's name. A lawyer can do that for a nominal fee. James, you're Will's dad and my best friend. I lost that once. I won't jeopardize it again."

"I'm the only boy in my family. If Will doesn't carry my name, then it all ends with me. That may not matter to you, but it does to me."

She touched his arm. "I didn't do it to hurt you, James. I just didn't think it through."

"I didn't think you did. I probably did a little over-reacting of my own, but I feel very strongly about Will having my name."

"Then we'll do it. We probably should go to bed. Six o'clock is going to come awful early," she said.

James grinned. "I've been waiting on you to say that."

Kelly shook her head and pointed to the door.

"You know, just about the time I think I've got things figured out, you go and change the rules." He turned to leave, then paused to face her again. "Just so you know, I'm proud of Will. I intend for him to know I claim him as mine.''

"He's so much like you. I hope you know what you're getting into.''

Crossing the room, James knew he couldn't return to the way things had been before Kelly and Will had come into his life.

This time with her and Will had shown him how truly miserable he had been living all alone...with nothing but memories of one night.

No, he'd never go back, never give up. One way or another he would figure out a way to wear Kelly down, make her want to stay.

Without him having to ask.

Chapter Nine

Kelly's feet hit the floor before Will cried out the second time. James had staggered into the room by the time she'd reached the crib. She scooped Will up into her arms and felt his forehead and sighed in relief. "He's warm, but it's not too bad. What time is it?"

James flipped on the bedside lamp and squinted at his watch. "Two-thirty."

Kelly did a double take, wondering if James realized he wore nothing but his boxers. She couldn't seem to look at anything but his naked chest. "It's time for another dose of medicine, and I imagine Will's thirsty."

James followed her to the kitchen and helped her give Will his medicine and a drink. That done, Kelly changed his diaper, then settled in a rocking chair.

She hugged her son close, drowning in the scent of little boy innocence, and closed her eyes. A few minutes later she sensed James's presence and looked up. Kelly couldn't help but smile when she noticed he'd slipped on a pair of jeans, but then sobered as her attention centered on the top button he'd left undone. What the man did for denim should be against the law.

Kelly did her best to ignore the way the dark hair swirled across his tanned chest and narrowed before it disappeared beneath his jeans. She blinked and stared at the floor, hating the heat that burned her cheeks, chastising herself for looking when she ought to know better. Forgetting they were friends, giving in to his rugged sex appeal was what had gotten her into trouble in the first place. Because, no matter what else James Scott might be, he was put together just right.

Against her will Kelly's gaze inched over the braided rug to where James's long legs were crossed at the ankles. His toes had a smattering of dark hair across the tops. She sighed. Even his feet were all sleek lines and sensuous curves.

He reached out to run a finger along Will's hand. "I don't mind telling you I'd rather face a charging mustang than go through what happened yesterday again. I felt so helpless, so scared."

She smiled and covered James's hand with hers. "From what I saw you handled everything just fine, even if you did cause quite a stir at the day care."

With a clarity that startled her, Kelly realized James really had done everything right. He'd sacrificed a lot to help her this summer. She'd zoomed into town, and he'd taken her and Will into his home without question. Not many men would go out of their way to help her after what she'd done. Sure, she'd had her reasons for keeping Will a secret, but now she knew it had been wrong to keep father and son apart. At least she had come to her senses before it was too late.

Despite all her arguments to the contrary, James had changed. Not that he still didn't worry her with his need to risk his health and career by rodeoing, but in all the ways that mattered, James Scott had finally grown up.

He'd more than proven that by being able to put up with a child as rambunctious as Will.

As for her son—well, he thought James hung the moon.

But then, so did she.

She'd always been a sucker when it came to him, even from the first day when she'd applied to work summers and holidays at the clinic. She'd never known a man more confident or cocky...or gorgeous. Heck, the man exuded blatant sexuality with each breath. He was every inch a small-town bad boy, a modern-day James Dean, a father's worst nightmare.

Maybe the changes she saw were all wishful thinking on her part, just because he'd said he loved Will and had every intention of seeing his son.

Kelly had accomplished what she'd come here to do. So why did she ache at the thought of having to leave? She already knew the answer to that. She'd loved him three years ago. She loved him now. And more than anything she wanted him to hold her... maybe even love her.

She sighed. Heaven help her. It was James who was to blame for this. He was the one who had kissed her, talked all sorts of nonsense, saying things she knew he probably hadn't meant. Because of him she couldn't seem to think of anything but him—the one thing she could never have.

If, like he'd suggested, they tried to regain what

they'd once shared and it didn't work, the consequences could hurt Will's relationship with James.

That was a risk Kelly wouldn't take.

Watching Kelly rock his son to sleep should have lulled James into a relaxed state. Instead it filled him with unfamiliar emotions so intense they scared him.

Every caress, every kiss, every stroke of her fingers against their son's dark hair made James remember when he'd been the recipient of her touches. How he longed for her to once more be the woman who looked at him with adoration, who'd come willingly into his arms, whom he had loved well into the night. He wished, not for the first time, that he could relive that night. If that were possible, he would hold her tight and never let her go.

Her sidelong glances and wistful looks made him wonder if she also thought of that one night, the night that now seemed a lifetime ago.

A sense of desperation settled about him. He knew it was nothing more than knowing Kelly's time with him would soon come to an end. Unless he could do something to make her realize he'd changed, she would return to school, insisting they remain friends. And that was something he just couldn't be anymore.

Kelly kissed the top of Will's head, then smoothed the hair back off his brow. She had taken down her standard braid and washed her hair before bed. The golden strands now settled loose about her shoulders and down her back, making James's fingers itch to plow into the mass. He drew its sweet fragrance into his lungs.

He noticed her somber expression, dropped to one

knee beside the rocker and placed his hands on her knees. "Kel, baby, what's wrong?"

She refused to look at him. "Nothing."

James lifted Will, now asleep, and placed him in his bed. After raising the side rail on the crib, he took two steps and pulled Kelly to her feet.

He leaned forward and pressed his cheek against the top of her head, then lifted her in his arms, unwilling to let her keep any part of herself from him.

"What are you doing?" she asked, her lashes dark against her pale cheeks.

"I'm taking you in the other room so we can talk without disturbing Will." He carried her into the living room and sat on the couch, refusing to release her, keeping her on his lap.

"There's really nothing to talk about," she said, letting her head drop against his shoulder.

He pushed several long strands of hair behind her ear. "Then, why are you upset?"

"Because what happened yesterday gave me another glimpse of the person I've become. I don't like what I'm seeing."

"I don't understand."

"In the three years I've been gone, I've killed myself. All the classes and the studying, trying to work and keep everything going, there's so little time to spend with Will. I didn't realize that until I came here where things had slowed down."

He tucked her head under his chin. "You should be very proud of what you've accomplished in so short a time. I hope one day Will realizes how much you've sacrificed for him."

"That's the problem—what I only just now realized." Kelly released a long, shuddering breath.

"What I've sacrificed to achieve my goal is what I covet most—my time with my son. Have I so completely lost sight of everything that I couldn't see what I was doing? With Will sick, I wonder if I don't have my priorities all wrong. Maybe I should quit school."

A thousand emotions rushed through James, everything from concern to elation. But of all the questions that came to mind, only one made his gut clench. Could he stand by and watch her throw away what she worked so hard to achieve?

He couldn't do to her what his father had expected of him.

Kelly pressed her cheek against James's chest, unable to face the censure she felt sure would come. "I've always tried to put Will's needs first. I just don't know how I got so caught up that I failed to see it before now, but I can't let it continue."

James leaned back and studied her, his mahogany eyes questioning, concerned. "I don't understand."

Kelly swallowed past the knot of self-recrimination that filled her throat. "I've all but neglected my son, something I never thought I'd do."

"Bull," James said. "No one has ever sacrificed more or worked harder to provide for their child than you. How can you say that about yourself?"

"Because it's true. Until this summer, I've spent very little time with Will. While I'm at school, he's at day care. If I work, then he's with my neighbor. When I go back to school in the fall, I'd like it to be different but I don't think it will. I want to get my degree. And I'm almost there.

"I had it all planned out in my head. I knew it would be hard, that I'd have to make certain sacrifices.

But I never realized I'd be virtually abandoning my son, leaving him totally in the care of others."

"You're making it sound worse than it is. You did what you had to do. I think you're being too hard on yourself because of what happened yesterday."

"I don't understand what happened to the phone. I had it with me and thought I had it on, but it never rang. On my way back into town I noticed my message light was on."

"You were probably in a dead spot," James said with a shrug. "It happens out here with the hills and valleys. Everything worked out. No harm done."

She couldn't face him, and moved from his arms to the window to stare out into the night. "No, James. Harm was done. My son needed me, and I wasn't there."

She felt him behind her before he caught her shoulders and turned her to face him, his eyes questioning. "I was there."

"Yes, but I wasn't."

His hands dropped to his sides. "Would Will needing me be so bad?"

Her heart pounded. "No." She'd only said one word, yet it had stuck in her throat. Even now, as she tried to deny her own need, Kelly longed to reach out to him.

"Since you got here," he said, "you've mentioned time and again what you thought was best for Will. Like it or not, I'm going to do what I think best."

"What's that?"

He raked his hands through his hair. "Tell you that the best thing for Will is for you to finish school."

"This is serious, James. It's about me being a good mom to Will," she said, emphasizing her words by placing her fist on her heaving chest as she faced James.

"I won't stand by and watch you throw away what you've worked so hard to gain. My son deserves better than that and so do you."

"James, please."

"When you're ready to go back, I'll take off and help you get everything moved to College Station. You've worked too hard, put too much into this degree plan to quit now. You're going to finish school. You're going to graduate, to be a vet."

Shock rooted Kelly to the floor. She stared at James, uncertain she'd heard correctly. "Why are you encouraging me to finish school, helping me move away? I thought you wanted to see Will, wanted us to stay around here."

James shrugged, his expression impassive. "I'll drive down on weekends."

"You asked me about what we'd had before." Kelly wished she hadn't pointed that out to him.

"I think Will deserves to have two full-time parents, but like you said, maybe it would be best for us to remain friends."

His words brought a keen disappointment that Kelly told herself not to question. It was, after all, for the best.

But as she watched James stalk from the room, she thought about his suggestion that they go back to what they'd had. If he only knew how much she'd wanted to agree, how hard it was for her to refuse him.

James had settled down and would take good care of Will should the need arise. If it weren't for her son, she would stay with James without any hesitation.

As it was, she couldn't take the risk that if they

argued and couldn't resolve the issues, Will would be the one to suffer the consequences if he lost his father.

She was certain she was right.

But then, she'd been wrong so much lately.

"You can't stay holed up here forever. You've got to leave Will sometime." James turned the kitchen chair around and straddled it.

Kelly ran her fingertip around the rim of her coffee mug. "Yes, I know."

"Your being here all the time won't keep him from getting sick."

She squeezed the bridge of her nose and sighed. "I know that, James. All right."

Her words came out clipped, harsh, and James knew it was only her fear talking.

She looked up at him then, and the anguish he saw in her eyes made his gut wrench. "I can't help it. When my son needed me, I wasn't there."

James leaned toward her and settled his hand on her knee. "Kel, things like this are bound to happen. You won't always be there when he gets hurt, and neither will I."

Kelly pulled her bottom lip between her teeth and frowned. "I've been thinking about that, too."

"What do you mean?" he asked, not following her train of thought.

"After the doctor examined Will, I tried to hold him, but he didn't want me." Her throat worked as she swallowed. "He reached out to you."

James shrugged, unsure of what to say. "Well, I've been with him a lot lately."

"I know."

"He was sick. It doesn't mean anything."

"Yes, it does." She pushed away from the table. "It means my son has made a connection with his father."

James watched her pace, remembering the surge of love he'd felt when Will had reached for him. "Isn't that what we'd hope would happen?"

"Yes, but it made me realize something I should have thought of before now."

"What's that?"

"Will's not a baby anymore. He needs you as much as he needs me. As he gets older, he'll need you more and more."

Pleased that she seemed willing to admit their son needed him, James wondered at her restlessness. "I've already said I'll come down on weekends. Nothing will keep me out of his life, Kel."

She paused. "No, I know you said you would come see him, but I stayed awake last night thinking about some of the things you've been trying to tell me. As much as I hate to admit it, you're right."

"About?"

"Will needs two full-time parents."

James stared up at Kelly, not at all sure where she was going with this conversation. One thing was certain—she had his attention.

"I'm quitting school."

James stood and gave her a long look. "I thought we had resolved this last night."

"No," she said. "We didn't do anything. You talked."

When Kelly tried to walk past him, he caught her arm and made her stay put to listen to him. "I can't let you do that."

"I could go back to college later, when Will starts school. I mentioned that before."

"I agree about wanting Will to grow up knowing he's got two parents just like we had. And I think that if we tried, things might work out."

Kelly tried to turn away.

He caught her arm. "What's wrong, Kel? What is it? I'm not letting you shut me out again. I'll stay right here until you tell me what's wrong."

She swallowed hard, her gaze finally inching up to meet his. "I never knew my parents."

He felt as if he'd just taken a hard fall, because it took a minute to draw a breath. Thinking back, he realized that, unlike him, Kelly had never shared any details of her past. "I didn't know that."

She sighed and her shoulders slumped. "I grew up in foster care."

He tried to keep his surprise from showing. "You never mentioned anything about your childhood. I guess I just assumed you had parents."

Her laughter cut him to the bone, because he felt the underlying pain she made every effort to hide.

"It's not something I bring up in casual conversation."

"I'd like to hear about it if you feel like telling me now."

"Why?"

"Because I...care about you. Sometimes it helps to talk about things."

"It's over and done, James. Nothing can change what happened. Living through that hell once was more than enough. I don't want to remember. Ever."

He slid his forefinger beneath her chin and made

her look at him. "You're the mother of my son. I'd like to know about your past. Will you tell me?"

Kelly walked to the kitchen window, her back stiff as she paused to stare outside. "My *past*," she said with a shrug, "would fit on a postage stamp. I don't have generation upon generation of family members who nose into my business or send birthday or Christmas cards."

She caught the edge of the cabinet. Her head fell forward, her shoulders slumped. "I have no idea who my parents were."

James didn't know he'd even moved until he pulled her back against him. A knot formed in his chest, as he squeezed her shoulders to let her know he was there for her.

"A sanitation worker heard a baby's cries and pulled me from a Dumpster where my mother had abandoned me," Kelly said, her voice wavering.

"Kel, baby, I'm sorry. I didn't know. I'm sorry I asked. I don't want you to have to dredge this all back up."

"No, it's all right. I've come to terms with it." She thrust her chin forward. "My birth certificate reflected only Jane No-Middle-Name Doe. Most of the boxes on the form were left blank, because there was no one to give them any information about me, no one who cared…at all whether I lived or died."

James wanted to comfort her but found words weren't adequate to express what he felt. So he held her, hoping she'd somehow understand.

"The foster care system didn't fill in the blanks, thinking I'd eventually be adopted."

Kelly grew silent then, and James felt the tremor

that shook her. He turned her in his arms and held her tight.

"Only it never worked out that way. My exposure to the elements took its toll on me. I almost didn't make it. That first year I was in the hospital more than out of it. Most young couples wanting newborn babies couldn't afford the expense of a child with critical-care needs."

James frowned, not sure he wanted to know any more, but needing to ask just the same. "Are you saying you were never adopted, that you spent your entire life in an orphanage?"

She shook her head, then gave him a shaky smile. "Oh, as I got older my health improved and lots of families took me into their homes on a trial basis, always full of smiles and empty promises, telling me to call them Mommy and Daddy." Kelly's voice broke.

He didn't know how much more of her pain he could bear. "Baby, don't—"

Her throat worked as she swallowed. "No matter how hard I tried, I never seemed to fit. The social workers told me I had grown difficult because of all the pampering I received early on. Later, when I turned ten, that label changed to rebellious."

James sensed that she'd put up an emotional wall. Her words came out flat and lifeless. He wished she would cry, release the pain he suspected she'd kept stored inside all these years.

"There was always an excuse, always something else wrong with me. It got so I refused to unpack my suitcase, because I knew in a week, a month, maybe two..."

"Where did you get your last name?"

"When I was fourteen an older couple took me into

their home to await my next assignment. They were both retired teachers." A smile tipped the corners of Kelly's mouth. "Do you know, they actually talked to me? At first, I did my best to ignore them. I refused to respond to their questions and tried to shut them out. But they wouldn't give up. They talked, despite my silence. I remember thinking they were senile. Finally one Saturday after they'd spent the better part of two hours talking through a movie I'd been trying to watch, I lost my temper and screamed at them to shut up. I'll never forget then what Mrs. Mathews did."

Kelly's smile widened then, and James knew that she was back in another time, reliving something he couldn't begin to relate to. "She grinned at her husband and said, 'Pa, did you hear that? Our daughter can talk.'"

Kelly bit her bottom lip, and her smile wavered. "No one else had ever been that persistent. After that, I became terrified."

"Of what?"

"That the courts would take me away, because they really hadn't wanted to put me with the Mathewses in the first place. They were considered too old to care properly for children. That's why they ended up with me—a kid nobody else wanted. It really was funny. They were considered unfit, and I'd long been labeled unsuitable for adoption. So for the first time in my life, in the most unlikely manner, I belonged. And I didn't want to leave. Ever."

James felt an immediate liking for the Mathewses. "So what happened? Did they adopt you?"

The profound sadness in Kelly's eyes made him wish he hadn't asked. "When they asked what I thought of staying with them forever, I felt like all my prayers had finally been answered. Only the system disagreed. Mr. Mathews was in bad health. They believed the Mathewses were too old, plus Mr. Mathews was in and out of the hospital. I guess they figured Mrs. Mathews couldn't handle him and me both. But I would have helped her with him. I cared for them both so much.''

James cradled Kelly in his arms, wanting to ease the pain she must have felt as a child and now. "But your last name?"

"When I took my first job flipping burgers, I legally changed my name to the one the Mathews had selected for me—Kelly Ann Mathews."

"What had it been up until that time?"

A tremor shook Kelly again, but she stiffened her spine. "Legally, it was Jane No-Middle-Name Doe. If I wasn't adopted by the age of one, the system was supposed to issue me a name, but I somehow slipped through the cracks, probably because I was in and out of hospitals. After that, every time I went to stay with a potential family, they'd rename me with whatever name they intended to use when they adopted me, so at one time or another, I've gone by just about everything."

James muttered a curse. He knew that she had said Mr. Mathews had died, but wondered when that had happened. "Did you keep in touch with the Mathewses?"

"I was too young to drive, and they were too old. We talked a lot by phone that first year, but then Mr. Mathews took sick and died. I ran away from where I was living to attend his funeral. I wanted to stay with Mrs. Mathews, but they wouldn't let me. After his death she had no one and lost the desire to live. She died four months later.''

"I'm sorry."

"You know, all I ever wanted was to be with them. They were the only ones who ever cared about me. I tried to be patient, telling myself that one day I'd be old enough to walk away from it all and go stay with the Mathewses. I was only with them a short time, but they loved me. I know they did. I just wish—'' Her voice broke.

"You can't blame yourself for the way things turned out. They sound like the kind of folks who took you in without expecting anything in return," James said.

"But I never got around to telling them how much I appreciated what they'd done for me. Or how I felt about them, that I loved them. I was afraid that if I told them, it might somehow jinx everything, so I kept quiet."

"I'm sure they knew without having to hear the words." He wished there was something more he could say to ease her pain, but there wasn't.

James had always thought he'd had it bad, living with a father who believed rules and rigid structure were the answer to everything. Compared to what Kelly had endured, his constant arguments with a father who had tried to make him into a soldier had been a walk in the park.

Kelly tilted her head back to look at him, her eyes filled with the hopelessness of the child she had once been and the love of two good people she'd been denied. "You're right. I don't want Will to ever know the feeling of not being wanted. I was wrong not to tell you about him. I'm so sorry."

When she'd left three years ago and he'd gone after her, he'd convinced himself it was because he was only worried about her as a friend. Now he admitted to himself that the night he'd held her in his arms, she'd made him feel things he hadn't expected or wanted to feel.

He had fallen in love with Kelly years ago, and damned if he wasn't falling in love with her all over again.

Problem was if he confessed his feelings and asked her to stay, he knew from past experience he could only end up hurting her.

Unable to get Kelly out of his mind all morning, James closed the stall door and turned as Cal approached. "This foreleg has healed enough we can call Pete to come get his horse. I think I'll make a copy of the treatment plan we used and take it to A&M when I go there with Kelly. I'd like to get them to look at my notes and do an evaluation study on it."

"I think that's a good idea," Cal said. "Others could benefit from your discovery. I'm not sure I'd have had the guts to take the risk you did. I'm mighty glad it worked out. So, when are you going to A&M?"

"I'm not sure. Sometime before classes resume." Sooner than he wanted.

"I had hoped you two might work things out and she'd stick around."

"She wanted to quit, but I convinced her not to." The way things were now, James wasn't sure there was a way to work things out.

Cal lifted his Resistol and scratched his head. "Have you told her how you feel and asked if she'd stay? Sara's always telling me men assume women know how they feel when they really don't. Women want us to put our feelings into words."

James shrugged. How could he tell her how he felt when he wasn't sure himself. "Kelly needs to realize her dreams. If I do what I want and keep her here, I'm afraid she'll come to resent me. Her goal is to finish college and get her vet degree."

"So, what do you plan to do?" Cal asked. "You going to let her walk back out of your life without a fight?"

"I'm torn between asking her to stay and encouraging her to follow her dreams. I just don't see how I can ask her to give up everything she's worked so hard for." And if he did ask her and she gave up everything, then what? Could he make her happy?

"You know, this whole thing between you and Kelly is stupid. What's important here is Will and what you plan to do to keep in touch with him."

"I figured I'd drive to A&M on the weekends to see him." Nothing would keep him from his son. Sometimes seeing him might be more difficult than others, but he'd do whatever it took.

Cal returned his hat to his head and leaned against the stall. "I've never known you to give up so easy. Usually a challenge like this would have you primed and raring to go. What's wrong?"

"Nothing. I just don't see any benefit in continuing to argue with Kelly. I don't want to burn any bridges." *Or make promises I can't keep.*

"Benefit? We're talking about your son. Not you and Kelly. That boy didn't ask to be brought into this world. You have a responsibility to him. I'd be making darn sure she knows what you want, what you expect."

"I've spent so much time worrying about what Kelly wanted from me that I never stopped to consider how everything affects my son." Trouble was James wanted to be with Will and Kelly, too, but how was he to know if that was what was best?

"Well, James, you're both hardheaded, but it's time to either figure out what happened last time to make her leave or else forget the past. Only then can you forgive each other. Maybe after that you can find a way to build a future together."

"What we've done to Will is no different than what Dad did, trying to make decisions about my life without regard to what I want. I've asked Kelly what happened, but she's never given me a straight answer."

"Speaking of your dad, does he know about Will?"

"No. I need to call him." It was one call he didn't want to make.

Chapter Ten

"Sergeant Major Scott here."

James's hand tightened on the receiver. It was time to lay everything out on the table. Past time. His relationship with his father had always been shaky, never the way he had wanted it to be. Nothing like the relationship he would have with Will. It was time his dad listened to him, time James made him listen. Long past time. "Dad, it's me, James."

"You didn't call last week. You worried your mother. I told her you were probably off gallivanting, playing—"

"Dad, hold on. There's something I need to tell you."

"You in trouble?"

James steeled himself against the familiar rush of anger. "No, Dad. Nothing like that. I've got something I need to say. I want you to listen to me for a few minutes."

"What have you done this time?"

James exhaled a slow breath, rolling his shoulders against the tension that tightened them. "I haven't done anything. Will you just listen for a minute?"

"All right, but I don't have much time."

Nothing new here. "I know I disappointed you because I didn't go into the service. The military worked for you, but it's not what I wanted. You never approved of my rodeoing, but I'm good at it, at least I used to be. You've never seen my place here in Willow Grove, but I have a nice spread, a house and the clinic. I'm proud of it all." He rubbed the back of his neck, trying to find the right words. "But that's not why I called. More than all my buckles or awards, there's one thing that I'm most proud of, and he's staying at my house with me. Dad, you have a grandson. His name is Will."

Silence echoed on the line.

"Dad, did you hear me?"

"Yeah, I heard. You caught me off guard. I didn't know you'd married."

"We're not." James didn't want to go into what had happened between him and Kelly, things he wasn't even sure he understood yet.

"I know you wanted to do the talking, Son, but there's a couple of things I'd like to say. Every time we talk, I get the feeling you think I'm lecturing you. Maybe I am. I order troops around all day long. I guess it's hard for me to realize you've grown up and don't need me telling you what to do anymore. There is one thing I'd like you to hear from me though. Your mama is the best thing to ever happen to me. I wouldn't be where I am today if it hadn't been for her."

James couldn't believe what he was hearing. "Things between me and Kelly are complicated."

"You used to like a challenge."

"I still do, but this is different. There's no easy answer, because of Will and partly because Kelly's going back to school."

"There never is. You made your own way and never needed to follow the crowd, but some kids aren't that strong and bend to peer pressure. What if your boy needs you?"

James knew his dad was right, but what could he do? "I want to be there for him every day."

"Sounds like you've got some thinking to do."

Understatement of the century. "Yeah, I guess I do."

"How old is the boy, anyway?" his dad asked.

"Two years."

"What's your address?"

"Why?" James asked, wondering if his dad planned to come beat some sense into him.

"I want to send him a set of fatigues and combat boots like you used to wear."

In spite of everything, James was pleased his father wanted to send Will something, even if it was the fatigues he had always hated. That threw him for a loop. "Route One, Willow Grove, Texas 76617."

"Be sure to tell Will they're from his grandpa. Will you do that? Maybe send us a picture of the little soldier."

"I'll send you a picture, Dad. But Will's no soldier. He's a little wrangler."

His dad laughed, surprising James.

He couldn't recall when he'd last heard his dad laugh.

"A chip off the old block, huh?"

"Yeah," James said, "I guess you could say that.

"Will you bring him to see us?"

His father was full of surprises. Any more and James might fall out of his chair. "I'll try to work something out."

"I mean it, Son. I hope you'll come for a visit and bring the boy."

A knot formed in James's chest. He couldn't bring himself to tell his father that when he arrived, he'd likely be alone. He didn't think Kelly would let him take Will for a week.

"I've got to go," his father said. "I know I wasn't around a lot when you were a kid and may not have instilled much in you, but I know I taught you to be honorable."

The phone line buzzed in James's ear a moment before he hung up.

Yeah, honor was one thing he and his father had in common. It was only one of the many things he intended to pass on to Will.

So many things had changed since he'd discovered he had a son. Good things, like him finally clearing the air with his father. And his dad listening. A first for them both.

Why hadn't they talked like this a long time ago? Maybe they had, but James hadn't been ready to listen.

He wondered if Kelly might have stayed if he'd been a better listener three years ago. It bothered him to think that with all the time they'd spent together, he hadn't gotten to know her, not really, not like he knew her now. Back then he never spent more than a couple of hours with any woman, except for Kelly, but she was different from the others. And he'd never had a serious conversation with the opposite sex, ever. Until the day Kelly had shown up with Will.

James realized he liked having Kelly around all the time. He liked waking up to her laughter and discussing the day's events over dinner. Hell, he'd even started drying dishes so she and Will could go with him out to the barn. He didn't even remember when he'd changed his routine, but it allowed them more time together in the evening before Will went to bed.

Truth be known, he wanted her to stay. But he wouldn't ask. She'd already had so many disappointments in her life. And he'd never been any good at commitment. If he asked her to stay, made a commitment, would he be able to live up to her expectations? God knew she had a lot of them.

Worse than watching her leave would be knowing he might fail her again the way he had three years ago.

Kelly laid her journal and pen on the bedside table and pushed the sheet away. The look of hurt on James's face when she'd told him she couldn't return to what they'd had before still wouldn't give her any peace.

Telling him no had been one of the most difficult things she'd ever done. Yet she knew a loveless relationship would never work. Not loveless on her end, but she knew James didn't love her. And she couldn't bear for him to resent her for forcing him to settle down.

The stigma of never belonging as a child had left Kelly riddled with her own set of scars. Scars she had never revealed...except to James. The way he'd held and comforted her had reminded her of the way he'd been before. It made her want to hold tight to him and never let go. But he threatened her resolve. And her son's future.

He was getting to her, and she didn't think she could hold out much longer. Being around him and wanting him was beginning to hurt more than she could bear. Tomorrow she'd pack her things and go back to school the way James had encouraged her even though Will would miss his dad. Truth be told, she would, too. She didn't want to admit how much. Nothing could have prepared her for the changes time had made in James. If she could have known how things would turn out, she'd have gone to him, told him, stayed with him...if he'd asked.

But three years ago he'd been a rodeo cowboy with a style like no other. And he'd gone all the way. Kelly wondered what had made him give all that up. Had she been wrong about him settling down? Had his dedication to the veterinary clinic made him give up professional rodeoing? Not that it really mattered now.

Kelly crawled from the bed and checked on Will. She hated to admit that James had been right about her returning to school. She really couldn't afford to quit now.

She sighed. Soon her life would be back on schedule. Barring any unforeseen circumstances, she would achieve her goal and graduate with a degree in two years, but this time she would cut back on the hours she carried and spend more time with Will. Once she established her own veterinary clinic, maybe she could buy a house for her and Will. The thought of a house without James didn't appeal to her. It would always be empty, never a home.

James. It always came back to him. It always had. She guessed it always would.

Knowing she wouldn't be able to sleep, Kelly retrieved her journal and pen from the nightstand and settled in the rocking chair. The nightly routine of writing the day's events in her journal was once again interrupted by thoughts of James.

Getting him out of her system wasn't an option. She wasn't a naive kid any longer. She wanted to lie in his arms once more before walking out of his life.

Just once more.

She paused, mulling the idea over in her mind. No. Absolutely not. It was the most absurd thought she'd ever had. A night of passion wouldn't fix a thing. Hadn't she already learned that? They had shared physical love once before and it hadn't lessened the pain of losing him.

But she had withheld the truth from him. Maybe if he'd known, he might have come after her. She'd spent the last three years wondering. Now, she wanted to know. But could she tell him that she loved him? If she didn't, how would he ever know how much she had missed him? She could tell him she cared for him, but would he realize her feelings ran deeper than friendship?

There was only one way to prove she loved him, the man, without all the trophy buckles and fanfare. It meant exposing a part of herself she'd never shared before. But was she willing to face possible rejection?

And if she didn't, could she live the rest of her life not knowing what his answer might have been?

Kelly opened the journal and began to write.

James heard a noise behind him and turned from the window. Kelly stood in the doorway to his bedroom, silhouetted in the glow of light spilling from her room.

Concern for his son propelled him forward. "Is Will okay?"

"He's fine." Kelly's hips rolled beneath her shiny blue pajamas as she glided toward him, shoulders squared, chin up.

She didn't stop until they stood so close he could count her eyelashes and smell the soap from her bath.

His pulse quickened. "Kel, I've been struggling to keep my hands off you. If you come any closer, I'm not sure I can. You need to think about what you're doing, because if I touch you, I won't stop."

Kelly's slow smile made him groan, but when he reached out for her, she planted her hand in the center of his chest. "As much as I've missed you, as much as the memory of that one night haunts my every thought, as much as I want you to make love to me again, that's not why I'm here." She looked long and hard into his eyes. "This is very hard for me. I've never much liked to talk about myself, but I won't leave again without you knowing the truth about me and how I feel."

He wasn't sure what to say or if he should say anything at all, but then he realized the meaning behind her words. "Are you leaving?"

"Yes. In the morning. Before I go, I want you to know that I love you. I have always loved you. Somehow I thought it should be so obvious to you, but now I don't think you ever realized it. You may not believe it because of my running off like I did before, but I did that for us both. Three years ago I didn't have the courage to tell you the truth. Because of my past I was afraid you might not care enough to ask me to stay.

But missing you these past three years has taught me that the silence is worse than the truth.''

James hadn't realized how desperately he'd wanted to hear her say that she loved him. He felt exhilarated and weak at the same time and wanted to shout for joy. Then he noticed her watching and waiting. He wanted her to stay, wanted to make a commitment, but if he did, would she blame him if he found he couldn't live by her rules? ''Are you asking what I feel?''

''Yes, I guess I am. There've been too many lies and half truths between us. All I want now is the truth. If you decide that you are ready to say three little words, then you'd better mean them, because there won't be any taking them back once they're said.''

He cleared his throat which had gone suddenly dry at her look of expectation. What could he say to explain how he felt, so she'd understand how complicated it all was? ''I...I—''

''No, wait. I don't want to know yet.'' The pulse at the base of her throat fluttered. Her hand shook as she gave him the blue notebook he'd seen her writing in. ''I want you to have this. It is more a part of me than anything I've ever given you. It's a journal that will tell you everything you want to know about Will. There are some things in there I'd rather you not see, but this time when I leave, I don't want to have any regrets. So, I'm laying it all on the line.''

''I don't want you to go. Can't we work this out?''

''Not unless you can give me a reason to change my mind. If you don't love me, I can accept that, I just hope you understand when I tell you I can't go back to what we had before. At one time I thought I could, but I've realized I wouldn't be happy without your love. When I leave this time, I'll know I gave you the truth and did everything I possibly could.''

He felt as if everything he'd been hanging on to was slipping through his fingers. ''You expect me to make a commitment knowing you're chompin' at the bit to get away from me again?''

''Yes. Because you loving Will isn't enough anymore, not for me. There's one thing I'm asking of you. If you can't do it, I can live with that and go on with my life, but I've got to know.

''I'd like your answer before I leave in the morning. I plan to take off at nine.'' She started from the room and paused in the doorway. ''Just remember one thing. Whatever you decide, I'll always love you.''

James dropped Kelly's journal on the kitchen table. For some reason he wasn't sure he wanted to know its contents, wasn't sure he wanted to know what had made Kelly look so sad the time he'd caught her writing in it. He pulled a beer from the refrigerator and lowered himself into a chair. For several long minutes he stared at the frayed edges of the notebook, then turned the page and recognized her neat handwriting.

To William James, my darling son:
After twelve hours of procrastination, you announced your arrival with a hearty set of lungs. I know that one day when you're older you may not appreciate hearing how beautiful and precious you are at this moment, but it's true. I know James would be so proud of you. He's your daddy, and you look so much like him with your dark complexion and hair. I miss him so much and wish he could be here with us. But you see,

he doesn't know about you. I wanted to tell him,
but couldn't. If he knew, I'm sure he would
come. You may not understand my reasons for
keeping the truth from him and lately I've had
my own doubts. I hope you don't hate me because of this. There were so many lies and rejections in my childhood. I was afraid to believe
James might be different. I let my fears blind me
to the fact that he is and has always been the
exception to my every rule. Though he may never
forgive me, he is a good man and will not hold
what I've done against you. My hands are shaking so much, I hope you can read this. I've decided to call him.

James leaned back in the chair and drew a breath
as the clock over the stove ticked in the otherwise
quiet room. He unscrewed the cap on the beer and
wondered at the ache in his chest as he continued to
read.

Will: I called James. I had so hoped things might
work out if he knew about you. A woman answered. I had thought I was prepared for anything. I wasn't. I hadn't allowed myself to believe
James might marry another and find happiness. I
can't cause him any problems. I'm so sorry, Will.
I wish—

The rest of the sentence was blurred from what
James suspected were tears because beneath the
smudges the paper was uneven in places.
He drew on the beer to clear the lump from his

throat as he digested what he'd read. Then he turned the page.

Over the next few hours he read and experienced, through Kelly's eyes and words, the joy of Will's first tooth, the first time he said Mama, and his first steps.

James had always recognized Kelly's strength. He'd known she'd had to be strong to survive her childhood. But he hadn't realized the true extent of her determination or her suffering until now. Her words, meant only to be read by their son, revealed aspects of her life she would never have allowed anyone, including him, to see.

In her writing she told of every milestone in Will's growth, but also she exposed parts of herself James had never known existed. Through her notebook, he experienced the extent of her love and also her anguish. But most of all he'd felt her loneliness.

He thought about what Kelly had gone through as a child and an adult and compared that to his own life. After leaving home, he'd chased rainbows as well as women for a time, but had never felt grounded, not the way he did with Kelly. Her childhood was riddled with pain. Her life since then hadn't been exactly easy. But always, except for her time with him, she'd been alone. Until Will's birth.

I caught you peeing on the bushes today. Somehow I think you must have inherited that tendency from your father. Sometimes I think I can almost hear your dad laughing at your antics.

James rolled his shoulders to ease the stiffness. He'd tied one on a couple of nights years ago, but he sure as heck didn't remember peeing on any bushes. He couldn't help but smile, because he had no trouble at all seeing Will doing it.

He thought about the things he'd learned about his son and the woman who'd gone through hell to protect and care for him. She hadn't told James because she didn't want to cause him any problems if he'd found happiness. Despite what her life had been like, she'd always worried about others and put their needs before her own. She was one hell of a woman.

Drawn back to the journal, James continued to read.

You got your first shot today. I was so proud. You were such a big boy and didn't even cry. You're as tough as your daddy.

James blinked, glad Kelly couldn't see him now. He'd never in his whole life been this close to crying. She had worked night and day to hold things together for their son. Knowing what she'd gone through while he'd been rodeoing for no reason other than pride and a stupid trophy buckle made him sick to his soul. Thousands of people had applauded him for eight seconds of daring. But nobody had applauded or been there for her. *He* hadn't been there for her.

James stared out the window, noticing the skyline growing lighter. He ran his hand across the stubble on his jaw, not sure he could stand to read any more, but there was only one more entry.

James, I wish I had the courage to tell you how much I love you, that I've loved you since the day we met. I loved you before we ever made Will. I love you because you ignored the barriers I'd spent a lifetime erecting to keep everyone at a distance. The fact that you refused to be put off by things that usually worked to put people off scared me. You are handsome, funny and carefree. You're everything I'm not and everything I long to be. I love you because you taught me how to have a good time. I'd never grubbed worms before daylight or gone fishing in fog so thick I couldn't see the end of my pole. I'd never watched the rising sun turn a frost-covered pasture into a field of diamonds or gone skinnydipping at midnight.

I didn't want to love you, James. But I do. I always have.

It suddenly became all too clear. James realized he had never felt worthy of his father's love. He'd spent his life risking everything to prove himself. But Kelly's journal revealed that she had never cared about the superficial—the rodeo, the trophy buckle or any of the glitz and glamor. She loved him for who he was unconditionally, and never asked for anything in return.

And what had shaken him most of all was that every page read, "I wish James was here."

The way James saw it, he had two choices: encourage her to follow her dreams and let her go. Or he could be selfish and ask her to stay.

He only had a few hours to decide.

No matter what, Kelly refused to cry. Her depression had nothing whatsoever to do with the lanky cowboy who carried their son along the corral fence as foals frolicked in the pasture beside them.

Liar.

It had everything to do with it, everything to do with him.

Kelly checked her watch. He was going to make her wait until the last minute to learn what he had decided. She leaned down to connect the horse trailer taillight wires to her truck. Heat rose from the ground in quivering waves. She ran the back of her hand across her forehead and wished she knew what James and Will had found to talk about so long.

Then, as if in answer to her unspoken question, the whisper of the hot summer breeze carried James's words to her.

"I love you, Will. I love you."

Kelly tried to ignore how rough and uneven his voice became before it finally broke, as if every word was wrenched from the depths of his soul.

James knelt on one knee and hugged his son.

She told herself to look away, but couldn't.

Will stretched on tiptoe and clung to his father's broad shoulders, pressing his face into the crook of James's neck.

A calf bawled, and Will pointed. James hugged Will again. Then he stood and lifted his son onto his shoulders as he had done the day they had picnicked in the backyard.

The morning sun shone down on the pair as James solemnly strode toward the truck, his steps slow, halting, his head down. Will sat pensive, wearing James's Resistol. It was as if he somehow understood he might never see his dad again.

Kelly had dreaded the time when she and Will would leave. Taking him from his father's arms was not something she'd wanted to do.

He still had five minutes left to give her his answer. She feared she already knew what it would be.

The sadness in his eyes, the slump of his shoulders, and the hesitation in his steps as he walked toward her frightened Kelly.

He lowered his son to the ground, retrieving his hat as Will ran for the water hose. James ambled around the back of her pickup, pausing to inspect the connection on the trailer hitch as he settled his hat low on his brow. His gaze skimmed over her making her all too aware of her rumpled condition. Sweat trickled down the valley between her breasts as she waited for him to end her torture.

His expression was guarded as he watched her. "I read the journal last night."

Blood pounded in her ears. "You did?"

"Yeah. You still wanting to leave?"

"Depends on you." He'd been insistent that she return to school, making it obvious even to her that he was itching for her to move on in spite of his love for his son. She didn't have to be run over by a wild horse to get the message loud and clear. Still, she had hoped that her declaration of love and reading the journal might make him change his mind.

Tension arced between them. She wished she knew what to say to make the situation less awkward, but nothing came to mind.

She met his eyes, and instead of the censure and unbridled condemnation she'd expected, she saw only pain, probably brought on by the loss of a son newly discovered. Needing to have this over with, Kelly hurried to the driver's door and yanked it open. "It's time. Come on, Will. Thanks, James, for everything."

He followed her and toed the parched ground, stirring up dust that settled in a fine layer over the dying grass. Finally he looked at her, his face like granite. "No problem."

She watched him, taking note of every detail from the sweat stains circling the band of his hat, to the way his jeans molded to his strong thighs, to the deep scratches in his boots. This was the father of her child, the man she had once loved. The man she still loved. This is how she would remember him...always. "Guess we'd better get going. Come on, Will."

"I reckon so."

After Kelly put Will in his car seat, James caught her arm. "You sure you don't want me to follow you to A&M?"

"No, we'll be fine." She'd heard James pacing last night. The dark circles beneath his eyes proved he hadn't gotten much sleep, but then, neither had she.

He pulled off his hat and fingered the brim. "Kel, I— You know you're always welcome here."

"Thank you. You can come see Will anytime." *And me, too.*

"Would you consider moving back here after graduation?" he asked.

She'd thought about it a time or two, because it would be good for Will to be close to James, though she wasn't sure how she could stand being near him, knowing he didn't return her love. "I don't know, James. I'm not sure."

James braced his hands on the side of the truck and looked at the ground. He leaned back. "Dammit, Kelly, I can't do this. I can't let you go without saying how I feel." He paused to draw a breath. "I know I told you to follow your dreams. At the time I said that, I had hoped your dreams might include me. I know you think I'm a thrill seeker. At one time I was, but I'm not anymore. Risking everything has lost its high. No matter what else you think about me, know this— I'm here for you and Will now. I'll be here in six months or six years. I'll always be here waiting if you ever change your mind.''

Kelly knew he would be there for his son, but needed to know how he felt about her. ''I know you want to be with Will—''

''Yeah, I do, but this has nothing to do with our son. That night back in May when you walked into the clinic, you gave me a rush no rodeo thrill has ever matched.''

She glimpsed the loneliness in his eyes and longed to ease his pain. ''I'm not sure I understand.''

''I'm saying I get that same high every time I see you or touch you. And kissing you carries more of a wallop than having a thousand-pound bull stomp on my chest.''

James ran his fingers over his jaw, then smiled at Will who jabbered nonstop. ''You said you wanted to give Will a home. Well, so do I. I already love him.'' He pulled Kelly into his arms.

''What are you doing?'' she asked, sounding a little breathless.

He placed his hands on her shoulders. ''What I should have done when you walked into the clinic. What I should have done three years ago. I can't let you go. I did last time and have regretted it ever since. This time I'm not going to be honorable.''

Her mind whirled. She was afraid to read too much into what he'd said. Still, she wondered if it might be possible for her dreams to come true after all. ''What do you mean?''

"Dammit, Kel, do I have to spell it out? I love you. I want to be with you, today, tomorrow and every day after that."

His words washed over her, sending tiny shivers up her spine. She couldn't do anything but stare at him.

"Would you please say something?"

"I'm speechless," she said.

His eyes burned her with their intensity. "Nothing is perfect, baby. Sometimes, you have to take the good with the bad, do trade-offs to make things work. You already know I'm no saint. In fact, I must be crazy, because I don't know if I'll ever learn to live by your rules, but I'll try. I can't promise much of anything beyond the fact that if you'll let me, I'll spend the rest of my life loving you and our son. Something gave you the courage to believe in the Mathewses. All I'm asking is for you to give me, give us that same chance."

Despite a lifetime of broken promises, she found herself listening, then weighing his words, almost as if she needed to give him time to take them back. She longed to run from the loneliness that represented her entire life and seek refuge in his strong arms. She wanted to believe they could find happiness together.

"I know finishing school and becoming a vet is your dream, and I don't want to hold you back. I want you to graduate," he said, running the back of his knuckles along her cheek. "But, Kelly, you're my dream. You have been for the past five years."

Another shiver raced through her as she considered what he'd said. She glanced at Will who fought sleep as his eyes drooped, then turned back. "Are you sure? Once we do this, there's no turning back."

When he didn't answer, she rushed on to say, "I'm

not questioning you exactly, but I want you to be sure. I know you said you want me to finish college, but how can we possibly be together? The school's in College Station. You've got your clinic to run. I don't see how it could—''

"Say the word, and I'll move down there," he said. "I want to be with you and Will. I won't ask you to give up your dreams."

"James, didn't you read my journal?"

"Yes."

"I don't want you to give up your job or the clinic. Haven't you listened to anything I've said? I've worked so hard to keep things going, but I've had little time to spend with Will. This summer with you has allowed me to rest and relax and see the way things ought to be. I'd like to take off from college a couple of years. Maybe go back when Will starts to school."

"Are you sure? I can try to work something out with Cal. Or maybe the college would hire me to teach. Though that thought is pretty scary. Or if you wanted, I could stay home and be a kept man. I'm not saying it wouldn't be tough, but, hey, if it would make you happy, I'd do it. I'll do that and more—whatever it takes. I will be there for you…always." He tightened his hold on her. "Give me a chance, Kel. Give *us* a chance to be a family, a real family. Together we can give Will a home filled with love."

Kelly couldn't believe what she'd just heard, and had difficulty drawing a breath. She knew he waited for her answer and she longed to say the words that would keep her here. Still, he hadn't offered her anything more permanent than living together. She wanted to be with him, but what if he later decided to leave, could she bear losing him? Had they come so far only to remain apart now?

James smiled. "Oh, yes, I almost forgot. Will you marry me?"

Kelly closed her eyes and leaned her head forward to rest on his chest. She smiled and tried to push away, but he held her firm. "You did that on purpose, didn't you?"

James lowered his head, giving her a kiss like none she'd ever had. It left her breathless and wanting more. His tenderness made it almost impossible to form a coherent thought.

James glanced at Will, who was almost asleep in his car seat. His eyes met Kelly's and held. "I've always known why I loved you, but until I read your journal, I didn't know what you could see in me. You weren't like most women. You're the only one who ever saw the man behind the buckle."

"How could we both have been so blind?"

"I don't know. You planning on answering my question?" he asked with a crooked smile that had always robbed her of every thought, except one. *Him.*

She struggled to appear serious. "Could you repeat the question?"

James captured both of her hands and dropped to one knee. "Will you marry me?"

Tears threatened, but she blinked them away and smiled at James. The time for sorrow was in the past. From today forward there would be no regrets. "I've spent so much of my life alone," she said, meeting his dark gaze, allowing him to see into that part of herself she'd always kept locked away. "I've never been impetuous. But I think—no, I know—you're worth the risk. I can't imagine anything worse than facing even one tomorrow without you. My answer is yes, most definitely yes.''

He stood, one corner of his mouth tipping up into a grin. ''I hope you're not going to want a long engagement.''

Kelly knew she shouldn't tease him, but couldn't help it. ''Do you mean like maybe waiting until this time next year? Texas with its bluebonnets and Indian paintbrushes is so full of color in the spring.''

''No way are we waiting that long. I'm serious, Kel. When do you want to get married?''

If they married this very moment, it wouldn't be soon enough for her. ''I don't want to wait.''

''You don't want to wait a year? Or do you mean a month? How about yesterday?'' His smile warmed her, but the unbridled love she saw in his eyes stole her breath the same way he'd stolen her heart years ago.

''Perfect,'' she said, and realized she meant it. Everything was perfect because of him.

He leaned forward but paused just before their lips met. ''I know how much having the Mathews name means to you. Some women today don't use their husband's name, but I want you to share mine. If you want, you could use both and go by Kelly Mathews Scott. I promise you'll never change it again, because you'll have my last name and my love for the rest of your life.''

Kelly leaned into him, accepting the kiss he brushed across her lips before pulling back. ''There's nothing I'd like better.''

''First chance we get, we need to go visit my folks. I want them to meet you and Will. They're going to love you both.''

A family. She had wanted James's love for a long time, but, since childhood, she'd longed for a family. And now he was giving her both. "How do you know they'll love me?"

"Because I do," he said as he bent forward to kiss her forehead. "I have one more promise to make you," he said. "I don't intend to miss any more firsts. When our next four sons make their way into this world, I promise to be at your side. It doesn't matter where or when, I'll be there for you. Always."

Kelly stared, not sure she'd heard correctly. "Did you say four?"

"Yes, ma'am," he said with a grin. "I always say exactly what I mean." He pointed to the buckle at his waist. "This is my last championship buckle. My rodeo days are over, so I'll need something to challenge me. I figure four more boys ought to do it."

As if Will didn't like having to share his mom and dad, he protested with a whine, then said, "Daddy bye-bye."

James unbuckled the straps on the car seat and lifted Will in his arms. "No, Son. Daddy's not going anywhere." He glanced at Kelly. "And neither is Mommy. From now on, we're going to stay together, be a family."

He caught Kelly and pulled her closer, the baby that had brought them together between. Then he bent to kiss her, leaving no doubt of his love or that he would get his way.

And that was fine by her. She surrendered to the enduring love and the family they had made, letting go of all her childhood pain and loneliness. She also let go of her fears and then finally her rules. She wouldn't need them anymore.

Because of James, the best-all-round cowboy and the man she loved, she would never again be alone.

*   *   *   *   *

**SILHOUETTE®
MAKES YOU
A STAR!**

Feel like a star with Silhouette.

We will fly you and a guest to New York City for an
exciting weekend stay at a glamorous 5-star hotel.
Experience a refreshing day at one of New York's
trendiest spas and have your photo taken by a
professional. Plus, receive $1,000 U.S. spending money!

**Flowers…long walks…dinner for two…
how does Silhouette Books
make romance come alive for you?**

Send us a script, with 500 words or less, along with visuals (only drawings,
magazine cutouts or photographs or combination thereof). Show us how
Silhouette Makes Your Love Come Alive. Be creative and have fun. No
purchase necessary. All entries must be clearly marked with your name,
address and telephone number. All entries will become property of
Silhouette and are not returnable. **Contest closes September 28, 2001.**

Please send your entry to: **Silhouette Makes You a Star!**

In U.S.A.
P.O. Box 9069
Buffalo, NY, 14269-9069

In Canada
P.O. Box 637
Fort Erie, ON, L2A 5X3

Look for contest details on the next page, by visiting www.eHarlequin.com or
request a copy by sending a self-addressed envelope to the applicable address
above. Contest open to Canadian and U.S. residents who are 18 or over.
Void where prohibited.

Silhouette®
Where love comes alive™

Our lucky winner's photo will appear in a Silhouette ad. Join the fun!

SRMYAS1

HARLEQUIN "SILHOUETTE MAKES YOU A STAR!" CONTEST 1308
OFFICIAL RULES
NO PURCHASE NECESSARY TO ENTER

1. To enter, follow directions published in the offer to which you are responding. Contest begins June 1, 2001, and ends on September 28, 2001. Entries must be postmarked by September 28, 2001, and received by October 5, 2001. Enter by hand-printing (or typing) on an 8 ½" x 11" piece of paper your name, address (including zip code), contest number/name and attaching a script containing 500 words or less, along with drawings, photographs or magazine cutouts, or combinations thereof (i.e., collage) on no larger than 9" x 12" piece of paper, describing how the Silhouette books make romance come alive for you. Mail via first-class mail to: Harlequin "Silhouette Makes You a Star!" Contest 1308, (in the U.S.) P.O. Box 9069, Buffalo, NY 14269-9069, (in Canada) P.O. Box 637, Fort Erie, Ontario, Canada L2A 5X3. Limit one entry per person, household or organization.

2. Contests will be judged by a panel of members of the Harlequin editorial, marketing and public relations staff. Fifty percent of criteria will be judged against script and fifty percent will be judged against drawing, photographs and/or magazine cutouts. Judging criteria will be based on the following:

   * Sincerity—25%
   * Originality and Creativity—50%
   * Emotionally Compelling—25%

   In the event of a tie, duplicate prizes will be awarded. Decisions of the judges are final.

3. All entries become the property of Torstar Corp. and may be used for future promotional purposes. Entries will not be returned. No responsibility is assumed for lost, late, illegible, incomplete, inaccurate, nondelivered or misdirected mail.

4. Contest open only to residents of the U.S. (except Puerto Rico) and Canada who are 18 years of age or older, and is void wherever prohibited by law; all applicable laws and regulations apply. Any litigation within the Province of Quebec respecting the conduct or organization of a publicity contest may be submitted to the Régie des alcools, des courses et des jeux for a ruling. Any litigation respecting the awarding of a prize may be submitted to the Régie des alcools, des courses et des jeux only for the purpose of helping the parties reach a settlement. Employees and immediate family members of Torstar Corp. and D. L. Blair, Inc., their affiliates, subsidiaries and all other agencies, entities and persons connected with the use, marketing or conduct of this contest are not eligible to enter. Taxes on prizes are the sole responsibility of the winner. Acceptance of any prize offered constitutes permission to use winner's name, photograph or other likeness for the purposes of advertising, trade and promotion on behalf of Torstar Corp., its affiliates and subsidiaries without further compensation to the winner, unless prohibited by law.

5. Winner will be determined no later than November 30, 2001, and will be notified by mail. Winner will be required to sign and return an Affidavit of Eligibility/Release of Liability/Publicity Release form within 15 days after winner notification. Noncompliance within that time period may result in disqualification and an alternative winner may be selected. All travelers must execute a Release of Liability prior to ticketing and must possess required travel documents (e.g., passport, photo ID) where applicable. Trip must be booked by December 31, 2001, and completed within one year of notification. No substitution of prize permitted by winner. Torstar Corp. and D. L. Blair, Inc., their parents, affiliates and subsidiaries are not responsible for errors in printing of contest, entries and/or game pieces. In the event of printing or other errors that may result in unintended prize values or duplication of prizes, all affected game pieces or entries shall be null and void. **Purchase or acceptance of a product offer does not improve your chances of winning.**

6. Prizes: (1) Grand Prize—A 2-night/3-day trip for two (2) to New York City, including round-trip coach air transportation nearest winner's home and hotel accommodations (double occupancy) at The Plaza Hotel, a glamorous afternoon makeover at a trendy New York spa, $1,000 in U.S. spending money and an opportunity to have a professional photo taken and appear in a Silhouette advertisement (approximate retail value: $7,000). (10) Ten Runner-Up Prizes of gift packages (retail value $50 ea.). Prizes consist of only those items listed as part of the prize. Limit one prize per person. Prize is valued in U.S. currency.

7. For the name of the winner (available after December 31, 2001) send a self-addressed, stamped envelope to: Harlequin "Silhouette Makes You a Star!" Contest 1197 Winners, P.O. Box 4200 Blair, NE 68009-4200 or you may access the www.eHarlequin.com Web site through February 28, 2002.

Contest sponsored by Torstar Corp., P.O Box 9042, Buffalo, NY 14269-9042.

Award Winner

MAGGIE SHAYNE

continues her exciting series

★★★★★★★★★★★★★★★★★★★★★★★★★★★★
THE TEXAS BRAND
★★★★★★★★★★★★★★★★★★★★★★★★★★★★

with

THE HOMECOMING

On sale June 2001

After witnessing a brutal crime, Jasmine Jones left
town with nothing but her seven-year-old son and
the building blocks of a whole new identity. She
hadn't meant to deceive the close-knit Texas Brands,
claiming to be their long-lost relative, Jenny Lee.
But it was her only chance at survival. Jasmine's
secret was safe until Luke Brand—a man it was all
too easy to open up to—started getting *very* close.

Available at your favorite retail outlet.

Silhouette®

Where love comes alive™

Visit Silhouette at www.eHarlequin.com   PSTEX